Angel
of
Death

AN ADDIE FOSTER MYSTERY

KIMBERLEY O'MALLEY

Carolina Blue
PUBLISHING

Where Romance is True Blue & Red Hot!

Published by Carolina Blue Publishing, LLC

ISBN: 978-1-946682-20-8

PRAISE FOR KIMBERLEY O'MALLEY

Death Comes in Threes

"This was my first cozy mystery and I have to say I absolutely loved it. Kimberley did an amazing job at keeping me guessing what was coming next. I can't wait to see what happens between Addy and Detective Wolfe cause something has to happen between them!

I also want to know who the man in Addy's dream is. And why those men were after her.

Can't wait for the next book!"

–Under the Cover Book Blog

"This was the first Cozy Mystery and Kimberley knocked it out of the park. I loved Addie and Grey and the two aunties. The detective puts out the vibe he is serious and hard core. But I am sure he has a soft spot for Addie. Hopefully in the next book we will see where the sparks fly for Addy and why these guys were after her. KUDOS to Kimberley for such a great read."

—Wanda Bridget Hickey, Verified Kindle customer

"This was my first Cozy Mystery and I loved it. I was drawn in by Addie and adored Grey. He was such a charming, funny and protective character. I can't wait to find out more in book two. This book is great for rainy days or a light read while you're on holiday."

— Author T. S. Petersen

Dyeing for Change

"Love Addie mysteries, but hate that they are such a quick read. And that I have to wait for the next one!"

— Amazon certified customer.

"Another action-packed book. Don't let it being short stop you from reading. You will absolutely love Addie and her BFF, Grey. They're hilarious. Can't forgot our hottie detective, Jonah. Meow! Trouble is always finding our Addie. She doesn't listen, at all, even if it's for her own good. She loves her dogs, and this book made me shed some tears because of one of her dogs. You can't go wrong with this awesome book. Read the first and then come devour the second."

— Sara, Amazon Kindle customer

"I am really liking this series! A nice, easy and quick read - just enough to take a break from real life and spend a lazy hour or so with a good read. Likeable characters and a continuing mysterious thread involving the main character throughout the two books so far - looking forward to seeing what happens in Book #3!"

— Vivian F. Shane, Amazon Kindle customer

Murder by Numbers

"Murder by Numbers by Kimberley O'Malley is the third book in the author's Addie Foster Mystery series. This installment finds our beloved Addie still dealing with her bad dreams, and finding it difficult to avoid trouble. When her estate sale book purchase turns out to be more than she bargained for, she has to solve the mystery before she winds up toes up. This series is full of quirky characters, mystery, and plenty of fun reading."

— Dee, Words That Sparkle

"Wow if mystery is what you're looking for this book has it. This is the third book and Addie seems to find things that get her into trouble. She love estate sales and she found a book that she thought was very different. After purchasing this book she starts to get followed by this creepy English guy who turns out to want that book and is threatening all her family if he doesn't get it. The Author keep you looking for clues and wanting to know how this is going to end. It was an easy fun read."

— TX Shadow

To my fellow Indie Authors everywhere. Thank you for the friendship, camaraderie, and advice. Keep doing what you're doing.

Chapter One

Addie walked down the dimly lit hall, unsure of her surroundings. She turned her head from side to side, seeking anything familiar. Each wall held numbered doors, like a hotel or a hospital. Yet no one else appeared. She rubbed her arms despite the warmth.

"Hello?" she called out and stopped to listen for a response. Nothing. "Where is everybody?" Again, only silence reached her ears. At the very end of the hall, faint light spilled from a cracked door. Maybe whomever she sought was in there. She made her way toward it, each step more difficult than the last. The hairs on the back of her neck stood on end. She couldn't name it, but something scared her, made her hesitate before the opened door. She leaned forward, trying to catch the voice within.

"There, there…no reason to suffer anymore. I'm here to help ease your pain."

The harsh whisper of the stranger's voice didn't match the comforting words. Icy fingers trailed down her spine. As Addie turned to flee, not wanting to know what lay within the room, a hand suddenly gripped her wrist. "Where do you think you're going?"

The chill of the hardwood floor under her back dragged Addie Foster from the nightmare's tenacious grip. She shook her head to clear it, ebony curls bouncing with the motion. Gracey and Lily, her two Shelties, washed her face with their pink tongues.

"Mom's okay, girls."

"I hoped we'd at least have a few months before this started again," groused a sleepy male voice from somewhere above her.

"It's not like I can control it," she muttered in reply. *He had a point, though.*

Jonah Wolfe, her boyfriend of a few weeks, slid off the bed, joining her on the floor. He took her chilled hands in his own, blowing on them. "I'm sorry. I know this is rough on you. Do you want to talk about it?"

"Not yet. Maybe over breakfast."

Gracey, the bolder of her two dogs, scratched at the closed bedroom door, then looked back at them over her shoulder, as if to hurry them along.

Addie laughed. "Ah, the joys of dog ownership. Or having a girlfriend with dogs in your case."

Jonah sprang to his feet in that

ridiculously athletic way he had. "My turn to make breakfast, so I'll take the girls out while I'm at it. Why don't you grab a shower? Scrambled okay with you?"

Addie stood, way less gracefully than he had, and stretched onto her toes to kiss his cheek. "Anything I haven't cooked is okay with me. See you in a few."

He left the room, chatting away to her little dogs, taking a piece of her heart with him. She sighed and wondered aloud to the universe how she'd gotten so lucky. Not for the first time. Not even for the hundredth.

Twenty minutes later, freshly showered and ready to face the day, the divine scent of pumpkin spiced something drew her to the kitchen. As she entered, Jonah grinned over his shoulder at her from the stove. "How does pumpkin spiced pancakes sound? Scrambled eggs seemed a bit ordinary for today."

"Delicious," Addie murmured, sniffing the air. "Have I mentioned how much I love fall?"

"Only every day since the season started. I thought you loved summer the most. Didn't you tell me that when we met?"

"Interesting choice of words, Jonah." They'd 'met' in July, right down the block from her home. When she found a dead body. Blood soaked her clothing when they 'met.' He thought she'd killed the man. "And when summer rolls around again, it'll be my favorite season. Again."

"Ah. You're fickle." He leaned in as she passed, kissing her hair. "As long as your infidelity only applies to the seasons."

"Of course," she replied from within the refrigerator. She bumped the door closed with a hip and carried syrup, butter, and juice to the table.

The girls pranced around the table, their faces pointed in the air, noses twitching.

Addie laughed at them. "Someone else is a fan of this time of the year."

"Gracey and Lily are fans of the smells of the season, I think." He joined her, placing a dish covered in pancakes on the table. "I may have made a few too many."

"What gave it away?" she asked, piercing two of them with her fork and plopping them on her plate. "You really should be training for Thanksgiving."

Jonah halted his own fork halfway to his mouth. "'Training?'"

"You've eaten enough meals with the Aunties by now. You should know better."

He dropped the fork. "More food than usual?"

"Give the man a Kewpie doll. Aunt Clementine and Aunt Beatrice use Thanksgiving as an excuse to pull out all the stops. And I mean all. They serve course after course. Thus, the need to start training now. Or maybe a few weeks ago."

"And by 'training' you mean eating less?"

He glanced at his forsaken pancakes, looking like a small boy who'd had his favorite toy taken away from him.

"Maybe after breakfast."

"Good idea. I'll get right on that." Shoving a large piece of pancake in his mouth didn't convince her of his sincerity.

"I'm not kidding. Ask Grey. Or Gertie. You can count on gaining a good five pounds between all the holiday meals."

"More of me to love," he smirked around another bite.

She threw her napkin at his head, which he caught with disgusting ease.

"We have time. Thanksgiving isn't until next week."

"Exactly! It's less than a week, since today is Saturday. You're a goner."

"Me? What about you?"

Addie rolled her eyes. "I'm a veteran. I don't need to get ready."

"Nice. You wait until now to tell me?"

"Yep," she said, flashing her own smirk.

"You'd think Grey would have warned me," he muttered around another mouthful of pancake.

"Nah, he likes to see you suffer. That's how you know he likes you."

"How would I know if he didn't like me?"

"You'd know." She cocked her head. "He didn't care for Noah."

"I never thought much of him either. Dating a patient…"

"I was a former patient, and he treated me for less than twenty-four hours."

"Still."

Addie muffled a laugh at Jonah's darkened expression and covered his hand with hers. "You just didn't like him because he dated me."

"Exactly."

A warmth spread throughout her belly. "*Was* being the operative word. As in past tense. And we only had five dates."

A grin that would do the Cheshire Cat proud spread across his face. "And you never…"

"I'm still going to kill Grey for telling everyone." But she wasn't angry with her BFF. Not sleeping with Noah made sense. She never felt about him like she did about Jonah.

The man in question glanced at the microwave clock. "As nice as this is, I have to get going." He forked in one more huge bite of pancake, washing it down with orange juice.

"First day back. Are you nervous?"

"I'm excited. I'm finally cleared for duty. Being off for so long was starting to make me stir crazy."

"It's only been a few weeks," Addie protested. Chills trickled down her spine at the memory of watching Jonah get shot right in front of her. Those hours spent waiting outside the operating room weren't ones she wanted to repeat.

"Hey. I'm fine." He raised his arm, flexing his hand. "Good as new." He stood, carrying his plate to the sink.

She stood also, following him and wrapping her arms around his waist. "I know. But I also know how lucky we were. You could have died." She squeezed him tighter, burying her face in his back and willing away anything that might ever hurt him again.

Jonah turned in her arms until she faced him, then he placed a hand under her chin, raising it. "I'm right here. And I'm okay." He brushed a kiss across her lips. "What I also am is late. I need a quick shower before I report to work."

She wrapped her arms around him, returning the kiss before letting him go. "And I'll be late, too, if I don't hurry. Be safe."

"Always." He gave her one final kiss before turning away.

As Addie watched him head into her bedroom, Lily and Gracey whined at her feet. She reached down and stroked both their silky heads. "Who wants to eat?" While she busied herself with getting their breakfasts, Addie thought about the upcoming holiday. Hopefully, her nightmare wasn't an omen of things to come.

Chapter Two

Addie opened the door to Smiling Dog Books, her small, independent bookstore. Doing so never failed to make her smile. This had been her dream for a long time. The reality was far better. She grinned as the girls ran behind the counter. By the time she caught up, they'd be comfy in their beds. Bringing her dogs to work was another fabulous perk of owning her own business.

She took a sip of her latte, also pumpkin spiced, and glanced around the interior. The height of Christmas shopping would begin in a few days. The crowds were no joke, but she was ready. Brightly colored book covers gleamed from every surface. Riley Larkin, a local writer of cozy mysteries, grinned at her from a six-foot-tall banner in one corner. The author, a close friend of hers, would be here for a few hours next Saturday for a reading and signing. Addie loved showcasing local authors. It was a win-win situation.

A frantic banging on the glass door dragged her from her thoughts. She turned to see Mrs. Henry, one of her favorite customers. She hurried to the door to let her in. "You're early, Mrs. Henry, but please come in."

The older woman bustled past her, talking a mile a minute while she gasped for breath.

Addie guided her to the comfortable love-seat in her reading area. "Here, take a seat. And a breath. What's wrong?"

"Oh, my dear, you have to help me. He's d-d-dead. You're so clever, solving those mysteries. I didn't know who else to turn to." Her reddened eyes implored Addie to do something.

"Who's dead?"

"Bill Hamilton, that's who. I told you about him. A widower who lives, lived, down the hall from me." She stopped, pressing a lace handkerchief to her mouth. "The poor man. Someone killed him."

Addie pulled over a chair after fetching her guest a bottled water. She sat next to her, patting her on the arm.

"Now, take a drink and then tell me everything from the beginning." She thought about calling Jonah at work; after all, homicide was his thing, but she decided to wait until hearing the full story.

"Well, a week ago, Bill went to the hospital," Mrs. Henry began. "He suffered a small stroke. One of those fleeting ones. You know, the one that comes and goes and isn't really a stroke. Or at least not a bad one."

Addie nodded, not really knowing but figured she could look it up later. "Go on, Mrs. Henry."

"Oh, yes, of course. Bill spent a few days in the hospital. Tests and all. And the whole thing must have scared him something fierce. He just wasn't himself. Kept talking about a 'ticking time bomb' in his head. He hadn't even made a pass at me. Imagine that!" She sat up straighter, indignation coloring her cheeks.

Addie stifled a chuckle. "I believe you mentioned he was sweet on you."

"Exactly! But since coming back from the hospital, he'd been kind of depressed. Down, you know?"

"It seems normal after what he'd been through. Tell me the rest."

Tears streamed down the elderly woman's face. "Yesterday morning, they found him in his bed. Dead." She buried her face in the handkerchief and wailed.

Not knowing what else to do, Addie rubbed her back. "Why do you think someone murdered him? Maybe he died of natural causes."

"No, he didn't. I know he'd just been ill,

but they said he would make a full recovery. He came to dinner with us in the dining room Thursday night. Had a bit of color back in his cheeks. And then dead. Just like that." She snapped her fingers in Addie's face. "Went to sleep and never woke up."

"I understand your concern. Still, maybe he did just die."

Mrs. Henry stood up as fast as her arthritis let her. "I expected better of you, Addie Foster. I thought maybe you could dream about it or something. Whatever you did when those thugs murdered Gwen." The older woman gave her a look over the rim of her trifocals that probably set many others in their places. "I guess I was wrong about you."

"I could call Jonah, uh, I mean Detective Wolfe. See what he thinks."

"I already spoke with the police." Mrs. Henry's tone told Addie how well it hadn't gone.

"And what did they say?"

"Not much. They may as well have patted me on the head. Said 'the old boy had lived a good, long life.' Can you imagine? I reminded that young man my taxes pay his salary." A chuckle escaped her. "Didn't care for it much, I tell you.

"I can't imagine he did. Let me give Detective Wolfe a call."

"I hope you don't call him that in the sack," the old lady said, with a cackle. "On the other hand, he does have handcuffs." She broke off in a fit of laughter.

Addie excused herself to her office to make the call, and tried without success to erase from her mind the thought of Mrs. Henry knowing about handcuffs. She sat at her desk and called Jonah's cell number.

"Hey, gorgeous," he said, answering on the second ring. "Miss me already?"

"No… well, yes, of course, but I'm calling on official business. Maybe." She sighed, wondering what he'd make of Mrs. Henry's suspicions. She relayed the story her elderly customer had told her, and waited for his laugh. Or dismissal.

"You never told me about your dream this morning."

Addie sucked in a sharp breath. *That* was the last thing she expected to hear. "Uh, no, I didn't. Why is it important?"

"What usually happens after you have one of those dreams?"

"What?" Then her stomach dropped a few feet. "Oh. Someone dies."

"Exactly. I'm not saying these two things are related. I'm not saying they're not either."

She chewed her bottom lip, thinking about the ramifications of what he'd just said. She described what she could remember of the nightmare.

"I'll be there in five," Jonah murmured before ending the call.

Addie blew out her pent-up breath. She was all for being an independent woman. But she also liked the fact that Jonah got her, and knew when she needed him. She brewed a quick cup of tea and went back into the store.

"Here you go, Mrs. Henry," Addie murmured, handing her the mug of tea. "I thought some seasonal tea might help. Detective Wolfe is on his way. He's very interested in hearing your story." She left out the part about his being interested after hearing about her dream. *No need to go there.*

"Thank you, dear. Sometimes, just having a nice, warm mug in your hands helps."

Less than five minutes later, Jonah arrived. His partner, Dan, was nowhere in sight. Thankfully. She wasn't a fan. Addie motioned to the sitting area of the store, where Mrs. Henry sat ensconced with her tea.

He sat on an armchair opposite her and took out a small notebook. "Mrs. Henry, Addie tells me you have some concerns about your, uh, friend's death. Why don't you tell me?"

Mrs. Henry pursed her brightly painted lips before placing her mug on the coffee table. "Only if you're going to treat me with respect, young man."

Jonah had a couple of years on Addie's own thirty-four, so the notion almost made her laugh. She cleared her throat instead. "I'm sure Detective Wolfe is more than willing to hear you out." She looked at Jonah. "Aren't you?"

He never took his eyes off the older woman. "Yes, ma'am, I am."

Mrs. henry stared at him for a moment, as if trying to decide whether or not to trust him. She then started talking, all of the details she'd told Addie coming out in a rush. When she finished, she reached for her tea again with a less than steady hand.

Jonah sat back. "Did Mr. Hamilton have any enemies, ma'am?"

"Bill was eighty-eight years old, Detective. Who would want to kill an old man?"

"Did he have any family?"

"No. Bill's wife, Mary, died years ago. They never had any children. He never mentioned any family to me."

"I see. Did he have any arguments or issues with any of the other residents at the home?"

"Magnolia Haven is an assisted living facility. There's a nursing wing as well, of course, for the old folks."

Jonah covered his laugh with a cough. "Yes, of course. Did any of the other residents have an issue with him?"

"Do I look like a gossip to you?" She fixed him with a look.

Addie jumped in. "I'm sure that's not what Detective Wolfe meant. It's just that you are very sharp, and I'm sure you know everything that goes on at Magnolia Haven."

Mrs. Henry sat a little straighter. "Well, I

can tell you Bill had an ongoing issue with George Baker. I can't imagine George killed him, though."

"Can you tell me about this issue?" asked Jonah.

Mrs. Henry's cheeks took on a pinkish cast. "Oh, well, if you must know, both men pursued me."

Jonah looked down at his notebook, seemed focused on it. Addie caught the subtle quivering at the corners of his mouth. "Thank you, Mrs. Henry, for speaking with me. I'll follow up with the facility director."

"Very well then, Detective. Thank you for your time. And you'll keep me in the loop?"

"As much as I can, ma'am."

Addie walked the elderly woman out, waiting until she drove off in her car. Then she lost it completely and laughed until tears rolled down her face.

Jonah looked up as she reentered the store. "So, it seems there may have been a love triangle at Magnolia Haven," he suggested.

"Stop," Addie pleaded. She wrapped both arms around her ribs, trying to drag in air. Finally able to breathe, she turned to Jonah. "Do you think there's any truth to her concern?"

"No, not really. But a few phone calls can't hurt. Besides, it's my first day back, and they're trying to take it easy on me. I'm bored already." He closed the gap between them, taking Addie in his arms. "And if there's the slightest chance this is related to your dream, I'm all over it." He kissed the top of her head and left. But not before petting each of the girls.

"And that is one good man, ladies. Mommy will be holding on to him."

"Talking to yourself again? Didn't I warn you about that?" joked Grey as he entered the store.

She stuck out her tongue at her friend by way of response.

"Very mature. I saw Jonah on his way out. Miss you already, did he?" He picked up her drink and took a sip. "Pumpkin spice, my favorite. Yummy!"

"Hey, get your own," she protested without much heat. She and Grey had become friends longer ago than either cared to admit. They'd been through everything together, especially these past few months since strange, prophetic dreams and a rash of murders had turned her life upside down.

"Jonah was here in official capacity, I'm afraid," she said then filled him in on Mrs. Henry's concerns.

"What aren't you telling me?" He stared at her for a moment. The smile dropped from his face. "You've had another dream."

"I noticed that wasn't a question."

"Nice try. When were you going to tell me?"

The hurt in his voice stabbed her heart. "This morning, I swear. It just happened right before I awoke." She told him about it, tired already of telling the tale.

"I've never been to Magnolia Haven. Do you think the inside looks like the place in your dream?"

"Only one way to find out." Addie took her cell from her pocket and hit a predial for Erin Mc Carthy, her part-time help. She had a brief conversation with the younger woman before ending the call. "Erin will be here in a half hour. She's happy to have a break from studying."

Grey rubbed his hands together. "We're off on another adventure."

"You don't have to sound so happy about it."

"Well, of course I'm sorry about her friend dying. It's just you usually do these things with Jonah."

"Oh, Grey." She threw her arms around him. "You know I love you. He just happens to be a detective, that's all."

"Sure, sure," he pouted.

She laughed, pushing him away. "Hey, we took you 'treasure hunting.' That counts."

His eyes lit up. "Don't think I've forgotten about that. I'm still looking."

"I have no doubt."

Last month, Addie had gotten mixed up in danger after buying some old books at an estate sale. The deceased owner of the estate had spent his life looking for buried Spanish gold coins he was convinced existed. Apparently so did others, as she, Grey, and Jonah were almost killed by a couple of murderous thugs, intent on finding the long lost, alleged treasure.

"Fine. But don't look for a handout when I'm filthy rich," Grey quipped.

"You're already filthy rich," she pointed out.

He smirked. "True. But when I find the lost treasure, I'll be even richer."

"As long as you don't let all that money go to your head and forget about us little people."

"Who are you again?"

"Very funny! I'm going to get some work done in my office until Erin gets here. Yell if you need me."

She opened the gate behind the front desk and whistled for the girls, who followed her to her office. Once inside, she shut her door and pulled her laptop from her shoulder bag. While it booted up, she thought about the dream. Nothing in it seemed familiar. But she did have a sense of having been there, or somewhere similar, before. Maybe it was a hospital or local nursing home. Ocean Grove boasted one small hospital, of which she'd already been a guest this year. As had Jonah. The hallway in her dream didn't resemble any of the floors she'd seen at Ocean Grove Memorial. She'd never visited any of the local nursing homes, although she had considered training the girls to become therapy dogs. Hmmm...that might get them in the front door.

Her computer sprang to life. She signed in before opening her browser. Curious, she searched for Magnolia Haven. The local elder facility came up right away, and she clicked on their website. The home page showed the outside of the building, complete with a courtyard that boasted a fountain and many shaded benches. Not bad. She scrolled along, finding out this facility held several different levels of care, from assisted living right up to skilled nursing and something called a memory care unit.

Mrs. Henry probably lived in the first, but maybe her friend had transferred after his brief illness. She'd have to ask her. Addie didn't know anything about these types of facilities, but Magnolia Haven seemed to have all the right accreditations. Not finding anything other than marketing, she hit the search bar again. This time, she typed in "Bill Hamilton."

A short obituary popped up. She perused the lines, nothing of interest jumping out at her. Seemed he'd lived a long life, most of it spent right here at the beach. He'd served his country in Vietnam. Nothing that made you think someone would want to murder him. Addie wasn't convinced her elderly friend was correct. Mrs. Henry might be traumatized by his death and not thinking clearly. But she owed it to her friend and loyal customer to at least take a look.

Lost in thought, she never heard her office door open, but she jumped at the sound of a male throat clearing in her doorway. "If you're ready, Erin just arrived."

"Don't do that!" She shook her head at her own foolishness. "Sorry, you startled me. Let's go."

Addie shut her laptop and left the office. "Let me put the girls away."

"Hey, Erin," she called to her part-timer.

"Hi, Addie. Thanks for calling me in."

"You're helping me out."

She led Gracey and Lily behind the front counter, giving each of them a dog snack. This week's delight featured doggie cookies in the shape of pumpkin pies. Her friend Gertie ran Any Way You Slice It, a local bakery. Known for her pies and cookies, Gertie also sold a limited number of canine cookies. Lily and Gracey numbered amongst her best customers. She patted each Sheltie on the head, laughing at the crunching noise coming from both.

"Erin, we won't be long."

"No worries, Addie. I'll do anything to avoid the hundred pages of reading I have to do." She glanced around the room, a wistful look on her face. "If only I could read what I wanted to everyday and not required reading."

"Don't worry. You will someday. Okay, we're off."

"I'll drive," offered Grey.

"As long as you obey the speed limit.

Driving with you is like being on the Autobahn."

"You've never been to Germany. And I like to consider them suggestions, not so much rules."

"As is evidenced by your ridiculous car insurance bill."

"Not my fault some cops are sticklers for these things. Hey, speaking of cops…"

Addie held up a hand as they walked out the back door. "No."

Grey pouted. "You didn't even know what I was going to say."

"Jonah is NOT going to fix any of those outstanding tickets you have." She waited while he unlocked the doors to his Jeep.

Grey slid into the driver's side. "What good is sleeping with a cop if you can't have the odd ticket taken care of?"

"I'm sleeping with him, not you. And I wouldn't ask him anyway."

"Ah ha! So, you are sleeping with him."

She gave him 'the look,' not that it ever worked on Grey. "A lady doesn't kiss and tell. We aren't all sluts like you."

He stopped at a red light, placing his hand over his heart. "You wound me. Or you would if that wasn't true. So, how is he?"

"Not answering. What do you make of all this? Am I jumping to conclusions?"

She glanced sideways at him, noting the teasing look had vanished from his face.

"Your dream makes this real. Or at least something. Maybe we'll have a better idea after we look around," he answered with a shake of his blonde head. "I need you to promise me to be careful this time." The light turned, and Grey started driving, eyes on the road, but he took her hand in his. "I can't lose you."

Chapter Three

A large lump formed in Addie's throat. She squeezed Grey's hand. He might give her crap, all the time, but he loved her, just as she loved him. "You're not going to lose me. Besides, when am I not careful?'

"Oh, I don't know. Maybe the time you broke into Gwen's apartment after she'd been murdered."

"Me? You were right there with me if memory serves. And we didn't break into anything. The door was open already."

"Which should have told us something."

She sighed. "True. I still feel badly about getting Jonah shot."

"That wasn't your fault. You didn't shoot him. For the hundredth time, Jonah is a detective. Getting shot is a job hazard for him."

"Still, if he hadn't come to protect me, and

you I might add, he wouldn't have gotten shot."

"He wouldn't have gotten shot if the bad guy didn't shoot him. But he did. It's what they do. Kind of like when a zoo animal eats one of its trainers."

"What?" Her BFF had a way of making his own logic in the world.

"You know. When you read in the paper that some wild cat in a zoo, or maybe a polar bear, eats someone in its pen. They always say, 'The tiger was just being a tiger.'"

Addie couldn't stop the wave of laughter that bubbled out of her, despite the grim topic. "I don't think it's the same thing."

"I beg to differ. It kind of is."

She knew this inane conversation might have continued on for another hour. Grey loved to debate things with her. The inaner, the better. But Magnolia Haven appeared around a bend on their left. She pointed. "We're here."

"Got it." He turned into the parking lot, then pulled into a space marked for visitors. "Do I have to go with you?"

"What? Of course, you do. I thought you wanted to go on 'an adventure.'"

He heaved a dramatic sigh. "It's going to smell bad. Like old people and death."

"Grey! That's a terrible thing to say. You're going to be old someday."

"I hope so. But I won't be living here. Especially after I find that Spanish treasure. I'll have scantily clad young men serving me my meals on a private island in the Caribbean."

"As long as you don't forget about me." Addie got out of the car. "Now, best behavior, please. And follow my lead."

"Yes, Mom," he griped but followed her through the front door.

Addie stopped inside the door, looking around. "Not at all what I expected," she whispered to him.

"Hello, how may I help you?" asked a gorgeous, young woman, stepping out from behind a desk in the foyer.

Addie fixed a huge smile on her face, all set to launch into her therapy dog cover story.

"Hello, darlin'," Grey replied, charm oozing from him. "The little lady and I have come to inquire about possibly having her dear granny stay with y'all." He turned to Addie, staring. "Didn't we, Sugar Plum?"

She resisted the urge to kick him. Barely. "Why, yes, honey bun, we did." She grabbed his hand, making sure to dig one nail into his palm. Hopefully he got the message. She turned to face the young woman.

"My grandmother really shouldn't be living alone anymore. But she won't come live with us."

"Too many great-grands under-foot, I'm afraid. This little lady just keeps popping them out, don't you?"

She should have kicked him. "What my, uh, husband means to say is that she values her independence too much. Doesn't want to be a burden. I'm sure you hear that all the time."

Miss North Carolina smiled, her perfect white teeth almost blinding Addie. "Why, of course, ma'am. Here at Magnolia Haven, we pride ourselves on structuring a living situation to meet each of our residents' needs. Is she still able to care for herself?"

"She is. We just have concerns for her living all alone in that big house of hers."

"Mansion, really," Grey said to the woman. "We don't want to brag or anything, but Granny is very well off."

"Well, our finance department handles that sort of thing. Let me get you one of our admissions counselors. She can give you a tour." She pointed to a comfortable looking couch. "Why don't you have a seat, Mr. and Mrs...?"

"Mayberry," answered Grey.

"Well, Mr. and Mrs. Mayberry, I'm Felicia. Please have a seat while I call Mrs. Audubon."

Addie latched onto Grey's hand, all but dragging him to the furthest end of the sofa. "What is wrong with you?" she muttered under her breath.

"Why nothing, of course. You know how I love a bit of drama." He scooched closer to her on the couch, placing an arm behind her shoulders. "Now, Sugar Plum, don't worry. I'm sure we can find a very nice place for your dear granny."

Addie snuggled her head against his shoulder, getting into character. "If you call me Sugar Plum one more time, I may de-plumb you. If you get my meaning."

Grey barked out a laugh before quickly smothering it. "Loud and clear. But that brings to mind a question I've been dying to ask you. What does Tall, Dark, and Dreamy call you?"

She was saved from answering by the approach of a well-dressed woman in her fifties. They both stood. The woman extended a hand to Addie. "Hello, I'm Sally Audubon. And you must be Mr. and Mrs. Mayberry. I'm so pleased to meet you."

Grey grabbed her outstretched hand before Addie could. "That's us, just like the old television show. I'm Charles, and this is my lovely wife, Petunia."

Addie really should have kicked him, but instead, she pasted a smile on her face. "Thank you for taking time out to see us, Sally."

"Of course. This way, shall we? I can give you a quick tour of our facilities before we sit down and have a chat." She started down the main hallway, so they scrambled to keep up.

"Why don't you tell me a bit about your grandmother first. How old is she? What is her level of independence? Any health concerns? That type of thing."

Addie jumped right into the conversation to cut Grey off at the path. Goodness knew what he'd come up with. "Granny Betsy turned ninety-two over the summer."

"And doesn't look a day over seventy-five," added the ever-helpful Grey.

"Yes, as I was saying, my grandmother is very good for her age. She loves to tell everyone that clean living is her secret. Only takes a multivitamin each morning. But she's slowing down a bit, and we've grown concerned for her safety living alone."

"Felicia mentioned she lives in a rather large house. I'm sure you're concerned for her safety."

"Well, maybe alone isn't the best word. There are servants there," added Grey.

"Oh, Charles, you do love to exaggerate." *Did he ever!* "Uh, what my darling husband means is there's someone in to clean and cook, things like that. But, she's alone at night. And I worry."

"Of course, you do, dear. Any loving family member would in that situation." Their guide turned down a hall and passed through a set of double doors. "This is our assisted living section. Here, residents have their own space and are able to maintain their independence. Each resident has a mini apartment of their own, complete with private bathroom, bedroom, and sitting room. There's also a small kitchen area with refrigerator and counter space. They take all their meals in the dining room with the other residents."

"Oh, that sounds lovely. Granny Betsy

would just love to be able to take her meals with people her own age." Addie lowered her voice to a whisper. "Most of her friends have passed on, you know."

"Indeed, I do. That's one of the tough parts of aging, I guess. Let's continue on, shall we?"

As Addie and Grey followed along, she peered around her, trying to see if anything looked familiar. She turned and caught Grey's widened eyes and shook her head no. Gotta love their unspoken communication.

Addie turned back to Sally. "Do you have any openings at the moment? I'm sure such a lovely place as this has a waiting list."

"We do indeed keep a list of interested, qualified potential residents. The wait depends on the, uh, availability of units."

Someone had to die, in other words. "Oh. I guess then there isn't any way to predict how long that might take?" She felt Grey grabbing her arm.

"Sugar Plum, maybe we should look elsewhere. Granny Betsy needs to be safe sooner rather than later."

Sally cleared her throat. "With the average age of our residents, the wait can be very short."

Although Addie understood what she was saying, it still left her with a nauseous feeling. "Well, maybe we could leave our information. You know, in case." She was going straight to Hell.

Grey rattled off his cell number before she could blink. Sally wrote it on a piece of paper.

"Great!" Sally exclaimed. "Now let me show you the gardens, for which this place was named. You're going to love it. Although it's much more beautiful in the summer."

Before they could stop her, Sally led them outdoors into a courtyard. The paved path led in a large serpentine, passing many magnolia trees and flower beds. A koi pond gurgled in the middle. "Why this is lovely. Simply lovely," Addie gushed. "Darling, maybe we should consider moving in with Granny Betsy."

"Now, Sugar Plum, where would we put the kids? And the nanny?" He turned to Sally. "Thank you so much for taking us on this tour. We'd like to wander a bit before seeing ourselves out."

"Oh, I'm afraid that isn't possible. We value our residents' privacy, as you can probably imagine. I'm sure you can appreciate that for your beloved grandmother."

Addie tried not to grind her teeth. They'd been so close. "Of course. We weren't thinking. Well, thank you again."

"My pleasure." Sally walked them around the building, shaking both of their hands before leaving them in the visitor parking area.

Addie stayed silent until they were both in the car and back on the main road. "Please don't ever let me end up in a place like that."

"As if."

"All she cared about was money. I mean, the place is gorgeous and all, but, well, I ran out of words."

"Now, now, Sugar Plum, don't get in a tizzy," Grey joked as he drove them back to the store.

"If no one ever calls me that again, it will still be too soon."

"You never did tell me what Detective Dreamy calls you in the heat of the moment."

"You're right."

"Ah, playing hard to get. Please tell me you don't call him Detective Wolfe."

A very unladylike snort ripped from Addie. "Only when he whips out the handcuffs. And that's enough of that conversation."

"Whatever you say, darling. What are you going to tell Jonah?"

"About?"

"About our little field trip?"

"Oh. I hadn't thought about it to be honest."

"But you are going to tell him?"

"Jonah and I don't keep secrets from each other."

"Ah, too early in the relationship for that?"

"There's never a good time for lying. Or keeping secrets. How about you and Jamie?"

"Oh, about that."

"No!"

"Yes."

"But I liked this one." Jamie had lasted longer than almost all Grey's former partners. Her BFF liked to think of himself as selective. And easily bored.

"Me, too. But he had to follow his muse. Whatever that means."

"Muse? I thought he was a stock trader."

"Who now wants to sculpt. And he can only do that in Italy, apparently."

"Oh, Grey. I'm so sorry."

"Me, too. I really did like him. But I didn't love him. Not like you love Jonah."

Addie wasn't sure what to say to that. "You've never loved anyone that way. But then, neither have I. Until now." She winced, not wanting to rub his face in her happiness. "Sorry."

"No worries. He wasn't my lobster."

She laughed at the famous television sitcom reference. "I think Jonah may be mine."

"Girl, what do you mean 'think'? We all know he is. The Aunties have been knitting. Blue and pink, just in case. Don't get me started on the names they've come up with." He shuddered.

"Thanksgiving should be interesting then. Poor Jonah. Someone should warn him. Again."

She sighed. Her maiden aunts meant well, and she loved them. But the constant mention of babies, not to mention her 'aging eggs,' grew old.

"Spoil sport. Where's the fun in that?"

"Very funny. I only just found him, Grey. The last thing I need is the Aunties scaring him off."

"Please. That man is a smitten kitten. Head over heels. He took a bullet for you. Two octogenarians won't scare him off." He laughed at her look of disbelief. "And besides, he already knows about them. Has experienced the terror first-hand. If memory serves, didn't they once ask him about the type of underwear he prefers?"

Addie doubled over, howling with laughter. "They did," she croaked out.

"And y'all weren't even sleeping together yet. I'd say he's here for good."

"I think you're right."

"Now, if we can just solve this mystery without you or him dying, we're golden."

Chapter Four

Addie waved goodbye to Grey as he dropped her off back at the bookstore. She'd promised to tell Jonah. Of course, she'd tell him what they'd done. She wasn't looking forward to it, though. He tended to worry about her. She stopped with her hand on the doorknob, a lovely, warmth spreading through her chest. Hard to believe they'd known each other only since the summer. Harder yet to believe they'd been dating barely for a few weeks. She sent a small prayer of thanksgiving into the universe for Jonah and entered her shop.

"I'd know that smile anywhere," crowed Erin from behind the counter. "You were thinking about him, weren't you?"

"Who? Jensen Ackles?" Addie laughed at her own joke. Her bordering on obsession love for the actor and his hit show was a running joke amongst her friends.

"Speaking of yummy. But I meant Jonah, as you well know," said Erin.

"Guilty as charged." She came around the desk and kneeled down to hug the wriggling bodies of her two Shelties. "And how were the girls for you?"

"Fabulous, as always. Who loves their Aunt Erin?" she crooned to the dogs in the voice most adults reserved for human babies.

"That's because you spoil them. But they deserve it. Don't you, girls?" Addie straightened up and grabbed a lint brush to remove the traces of dog hair they'd left behind. "How was business?"

"Really good. I think people are finally starting to remember Christmas arrives next month." Erin gestured to the dozen or so people milling about the store. "You might want to check inventory for the children's section. We enjoyed a real run in there today."

"Music to my ears. Hey, I'm back for the rest of the day if you want to take off. Or you can stay if you want. I can always find things to do in the store."

"If you don't mind, I might stay a bit longer. Make it worth my while."

"And avoid studying, right?"

"You caught me. But I will be studying the rest of the weekend. Unless you need me tomorrow…"

Addie laughed and headed for her office.

"Stay awhile, then. Let me know when you're leaving. And I have tomorrow covered."

"Yes, Boss," Erin replied with a sassy salute.

Addie shook her head and headed to the coffee maker in her office, rubbing her temples as she went. The nightmare must have messed with her sleep. The faintest of dull aches had started behind her eyes.

Several hours later, she started at the sound of someone at her door. She looked up to see Erin standing there. "Sorry. Were you there long?"

"Nope. Leaving now, so I came to let you know." She gestured to the backpack slung over her shoulder. "This stuff isn't going to study itself you know. Too busy today to even bother taking out a book."

"Hooray! That's good news for me. Thanks again for coming." She stood and followed Erin to the front of the store.

"Oh, I took the girls out for a potty break about fifteen minutes ago. They have fresh water, so they should be good."

"Aw, thanks, Erin. Be safe going home."

"I will. See you next week."

Addie said a quick hello to the girls before a customer approached her. And then another. Before she knew it, time had flown, and she was tidying up the shop for closing. She preferred to keep it ship shape so she wouldn't have to do any last-minute cleaning before opening the next morning. At least on Sundays, she didn't open until eleven.

Her phone rang, the opening line of "I'm Too Sexy" blaring from her pocket. Her pulse kicked up. Jonah. Grey took delight in regularly high-jacking her phone and inserting very specific ringtones for folks.

"Hey," she answered before it went to voicemail. Looking around, she noticed only an older couple in the back, so she ducked behind the counter and perched on the stool.

"Hey, yourself. How's your day been?"

She crossed her fingers before answering. "Fine. Good day for the store. How was yours?" She hadn't technically lied, and she would tell him as soon as she saw him. But not over the phone.

"Boring. Never thought I'd say that. But it's good to be back."

"What? You didn't enjoy hanging out with me and the girls in the thrilling world of retail?"

"Not to mention hours of painful rehab to be endured."

"Oh, yeah." Addie winced. Jonah had indeed suffered through weeks of therapy for his arm, often coming home and standing in a hot shower to relieve the aches and pains. "Sorry."

"It's all good. I'm back to full usage. And you know I love hanging out with you." His gravelly voice lowered on that last bit, sending shivers up her spine.

"Good answer," she joked.

"Are you closing up soon?"

"I am. I'll be on time. What were you thinking for dinner? Thai? Italian? Mexican? Stay in? Go out?" She stopped and shook her head. They sounded like an old married couple.

"How about I surprise you. Go home, take a hot shower or bath, and I'll grab something. How does that sound?"

"Like I'm the luckiest woman in the world."

"Nah, only the prettiest. See you soon."

She held the phone after he disconnected, waiting for her pulse to slow. She *was* the luckiest woman alive. The grin stayed on her face as she tidied up and finally locked the front door after the last customer left. She whistled for the girls, who were enjoying an extended siesta behind the desk. Like a synchronized swim team, both dogs bowed to the floor, stretching their legs and backs.

"You're so cute I can't stand it." She rubbed both fluffy heads before attaching leashes and grabbing her things.

Addie whistled off-key all the way home, her happy mood staying with her. She'd be taking that hot bath. And maybe showcasing some of the new lingerie she'd purchased. Jonah could be as lucky as she.

Her smile faded as she pulled into her driveway. A white envelope hung on her storm door. She turned off the car and didn't move, squelching the impulse to run up and rip it open. Nothing had arrived in weeks from her 'secret admirer,' as Grey liked to joke. Actually, after the giant bear at her store doorstep, no one joked anymore.

She closed her eyes before reaching for her phone. Hitting a preset, she waited as it rang in her car. Gracey must have picked up her mood, as she let out a half-moan, half-howl from the back.

"Hey, couldn't wait to talk to me? I'm leaving the station now."

"Can you skip the food? Come right home? Please."

Something in her voice must have tipped Jonah off. "What happened?"

"Not sure. It may be nothing."

"But it's something or you wouldn't have called."

She heard the sound of his car door closing. She sagged back against the seat. Only less than ten minutes away now. "There's something on my porch. An envelope taped to the door. I didn't open it." A half sob ripped from her throat. "Heck, I didn't even leave the car."

"Good girl. Stay there, I'm coming."

He continued to talk to her about nothing and everything as she sat, staring at the offending envelope. How naïve she'd been, thinking her would-be suitor had gotten bored. Given up. The slow, deep sound of Jonah's voice soothed her fragile nerves. Her pulse slowed a bit. After a few minutes, his car turned onto her block. She exhaled her pent-up breath and disconnected the phone. "Girls, stay here for a moment. I'll be right back."

She jumped out of the car, throwing herself into his arms as Jonah exited his car. "Thank you for hurrying. Thank you for everything."

He smiled down into her face for a moment. "Anything for you." He kissed her before pulling on latex gloves. "Stay here."

She followed him to the edge of her porch. "Why? Do you think it might explode?"

Jonah shook his head, a lock of dark hair falling across his forehead. "No. He's been very low tech so far. But better safe than sorry."

"Wouldn't safe include you as well?" The thought of him being hurt again, because of her, slithered like a poisonous snake through her gut.

"Addie, I'm not taking any chances with your safety. I'll look before I open."

She nodded and stood where she was as he walked to the door. With one gloved hand, Jonah removed the envelope from the door, turning it over to inspect it. "I don't see anything suspicious." He removed a penknife from his pocket and slit it open, taking out a single sheet of white paper.

Addie clenched her hands into fists at her side as his expression darkened. "Tell me," she whispered, unable to raise her voice over the fear lodged in her throat.

He sat on the porch swing, patting the cushion next to him. She approached on wooden legs, dreading what she was about to see. Jonah pulled a clear evidence bag from his pocket and slid the paper and envelope inside before sealing it.

"You don't have to read it," he advised.

She sank into the swing next to him, hands shaking as she reached for the bag. "I do. I need to know."

Jonah nodded before holding out the paper for her to see.

My love for you remains pure. Sadly, I cannot say the same for you, Adelaide Foster. My gifts went unappreciated while you turned to HIM. You will be sorry. So will he.

"Oh," she gasped between the hands covering her mouth. Lunch had been hours ago, but the salad threatened to come up. She turned to Jonah. "What are we going to do?"

"First, we go inside." He thrust his keys at her. She'd given him a key to her house a few weeks back. "Go, now. I'll get the girls."

His tone didn't allow for argument. She rushed to the door, almost dropping his keys as she tried to open it. She heard the sound of her car door opening and his voice as he talked to the girls. The thought of this unknown man threatening Jonah drove her to the powder room. Kneeling before the commode, she dry-heaved as she sobbed. This wasn't fair. Their lives were just getting back on track, settling down.

A moment later, she felt his hands in her hair, holding back her wild curls. "I'm right here, Addie. No one is going to hurt you. I promise."

"I don't care about that. What about you? How do I keep you safe?" She turned and buried her face into his chest. "I almost lost you once, Jonah. I can't go through that again."

He held her tightly, murmuring softly as she clung to him. Gracey and Lily crowded into the tiny powder room, pushing their noses against Addie. "Nothing is going to happen to either of us. Do you hear me?" He waited until she nodded against his chest. "I won't let it."

She straightened up, dashing away the remaining tears from her face. "But how, Jonah? How will you keep us safe? We don't even know who he is."

He dragged a hand through his short, dark hair. "I'll figure it out." He laughed at her frown. "Okay, we'll figure this out."

"I like the sound of we." She reached up and kissed his cheek. "What do we do about the letter?"

"I'll take it to the station. Won't take me long. In fact, why don't you come along? I'd feel better knowing you weren't here alone."

"Normally, I might fight you on this. Not right now. Let me take care of the girls first." She headed out to the kitchen to get their dinners.

"Don't get your hopes up," he warned.

"So far, he's been very careful not to leave any trace."

"Maybe he got lazy this time. A girl can hope." She smiled at him but didn't feel it. This stalker of hers was getting old. She wanted it over. Done. She wanted to move on with Jonah. They spent most of their time together these days. More often than not, he stayed at her place. It was easier with the dogs. Life with him felt…well, normal. She could be herself. He'd already seen her at her worst. At least she hoped.

"Ready?" Jonah stood by the door, evidence bag in his hand.

Addie shuddered at the thought of some unknown person writing that. Sending it to her. Threatening them. Then a terrible thought occurred to her. She stopped in front of him. "Do you think I know this person?" She pointed at the clear evidence bag, her hand shaking. "Could someone I actually know have sent that to me?"

I don't know, honey. Maybe." He followed her out and waited while she locked the door. "There's no way to tell yet."

She glanced around her quiet block. "I want to feel safe again, Jonah. I want to believe you're safe as well."

He threw an arm around her shoulders as they walked to the car. "I know. Me, too."

She liked that he wasn't throwing out false platitudes just to make her feel safe. She preferred honesty, even if it didn't comfort her so much.

Chapter Five

Several hours later Jonah pulled back into her driveway. They'd meant to drop off the letter and leave, but the nature of the threat escalated her case. What was once considered a harmless flirtation by his boss had become a legitimate threat to be taken seriously, especially since the offender named Jonah in his note, threatening him.

"I still have to call Grey. He'll want to know."

"Agreed. But maybe tomorrow?" He rubbed his shoulder as they got out of the car. "Not sure I can handle him tonight."

"Are you in pain?" Addie cringed, thinking about dragging him into yet another of her problems.

"No, not really. I'm tired more than anything." Jonah smiled at her. "Not used to putting in a full day again."

"A fuller one thanks to me," she muttered.

"Hey. This is not your fault." He stood before her and lifted her chin with one finger. "Do you hear me? You did not do anything wrong."

"And yet, here we are. Again. And then there's the dream."

He blew out a long breath. "Right. The dream. Why don't you tell me about it?"

"Let's eat. I can tell you then." She grabbed plates while Jonah took the girls out back to relieve their bladders. When he came back, she was sitting at the table dishing up the Chinese food they'd gotten on the way home. Chicken and broccoli for her. Orange beef for him. He pulled out the opposite chair and sat.

Gracey let out a soft woof, circling the table with her twitching nose held high. Lily, the less subtle of the two, crossed to Jonah and leaned against him, all the while looking up at him with her soulful dark eyes.

"Somebody's got your number," Addie commented. She melted a bit as he reached down to caress her dog's silky face.

"Can't help it if I'm a sucker for small, furry dogs. And the beautiful woman who owns them." He dished out a helping of the beef before adding a bit of her chicken. "Now, tell me."

Addie did, breathing slowly and deeply

to fight off the chills creeping across her flesh at the memory. She took a first bite of her favorite Chinese dish, and then she told him what she and Grey had done.

Jonah shook his head before putting down his fork. "Why am I not surprised? And what did you find?"

She cocked her head. "You're not angry?"

"Not sure angry is the right word."

"How about frustrated, scared, or wanting to lock me in a closet?"

"That last one isn't one word but works. Look, I know you want to figure these things out, and I can't imagine what you go through with these dreams."

"But? There was definitely a but in there."

"But I need you to be careful, Addie. To take these things seriously."

"I do, Jonah. I promise. Besides, we went to a senior home in broad daylight. What could have happened?"

His short bark of laughter was far from comforting. "What indeed? Did the place look familiar?"

"No, I didn't see anything from my dream. But we didn't get to see all of it. There's a wing for the more, uh, sick or maybe elderly, residents. I asked to see it, but she shot me down, claiming privacy laws and all that."

Jonah leaned back in his chair. "How did you get her to take you on a tour in the first place? It's not like either one of you is old enough to consider living there."

She ignored the heat creeping into her cheeks. "We pretended to be a married couple. Mr. and Mrs. Mayberry, if you can believe it. Grey's idea."

"Something you're not telling me?"

She appreciated his attempt at levity. "Very funny. He told the woman we were looking for a place for my Grandmother Betsy."

"At least you didn't say the Aunties. They'd have skinned you alive."

"You're not kidding. I may have been banned from Thanksgiving dinner. Knowing them, though, they'd probably still be knitting booties." She slapped a hand over her mouth as soon as she uttered those words.

A dark eyebrow, the one with the scar running through it, climbed toward Jonah's hairline. "No pressure there," he quipped.

"I'm so sorry. I didn't mean to mention that bit."

To her shock, he roared with laughter. "Are you kidding me? They asked me about my choice in underwear and sperm count at practically our first meeting. Nothing about those two could shock me."

She shuddered. "Never tell them. They'd take it as a challenge."

"Duly noted. But seriously, I do want kids, someday. You know that. And neither of us is getting any younger."

"Thanks…I think. What are you saying?"

"Nothing. Not yet at least. I'm an old-fashioned kind of guy. There will be a question before any of that happens." He took another bite of his dinner, washing it down with some water.

She watched him eat, amazed at his ability to do so. As if he hadn't just mentioned marriage and children. "Uh... what just happened?"

He grinned at her. Grinned! "Never thought I'd make you speechless."

"How can you talk about such things, so casually, with all that's going on?" Addie's mind whirled at the thought.

"Life is short, Addie. And since I've known you, there's always been something 'going on.' Just saying."

"Okay, true, but it was never a threat to both of us. Aren't you taking this seriously? I need you to take this seriously." She cringed at the screechy note her voice had taken on, somewhere in the range of fish wife, but she could do nothing about it.

Jonah's chocolate eyes darkened to black. "I take it very seriously. This needs to end. This person who thinks he can threaten you has to stop. And pay for his actions. But none of that changes how I feel about you, Addie Foster. I hope you know that."

She nodded, knowing words couldn't make their way past the lump in her throat. She stood up and closed the distance between them, throwing her arms around him where he sat. Her tears streaked down her face and into his hair. "I cannot lose you," she whispered.

Jonah stood, never letting go of her. "I'm right here. With you. I'm not going anywhere, and no one is going to hurt me. Or you." He led her to the sofa, their dinners abandoned.

"I'm sorry," she sobbed against his chest.

"You have nothing to be sorry for." He rubbed her back while she pulled herself together. "Now I need you to focus. Think, Addie. Who could this be?"

"I don't know. I get that everyone wants to point the finger at Noah, but I really don't think so."

"Tell me why."

She struggled to put her thoughts into words. "Noah didn't care enough about me to stalk me after I broke up with him. He wasn't, uh, passionate enough to go to the trouble." She wrung her hands, hoping he understood what she meant.

"You told me he was very upset when you broke it off with him."

Addie sighed, wiping away the remaining tears from her face. "Upset, yes. But honestly, I think it was more about my doing it in a public place than anything. He was embarrassed, left me sitting there."

"Yeah, real nice guy. But I agree with you. I don't think it's him either. But I wanted it to be him," he growled.

"Now, now, you won in the end." His jealous tone did a funny little thing to her heart, causing it to flip in her chest.

"True." His smile was all teeth, not unlike his namesake. "So, who else then? Think. Anyone who paid a little more attention than they should have. Made you feel in anyway uncomfortable."

She closed her eyes, concentrating on the past few months. Nothing came to mind other than the obvious criminals she'd had dealings with. She opened her eyes and stared at him. "I can't think of anyone, Jonah. You know how crazy my life has been these past few months. Nothing else springs to mind. Are you sure I would know him? Or her?"

"About seventy percent of stalking victims know their stalker, at least superficially. It's possible you don't. It could be someone who came in the store. Or even someone you bumped into in the coffee shop or on the street."

"This is a small town. People pretty much know each other. I can't imagine it's someone I've known all my life. Why now?"

"You could be right. It may be someone who's new to town or someone who doesn't live here in Ocean Grove but maybe work brings them here."

"That narrows it down a bit. This is a beach town. The population swells from May through October."

"True, but this is continuing. And he's

leaving stuff at your house. He knows his way around and is most likely local."

"I thought he'd given up. Gotten over me. Things were quiet for a while. Wishful thinking, I guess."

Lily whined and pressed her furry body against Addie's legs. She picked up her dog and hugged her tightly. "It's okay. Or it will be." She stroked the dog's head, hoping her words were correct.

Gracey, not to be outdone by her sister, sat on Jonah's feet, placing one white paw on his knee. "You're a good girl," he crooned to her dog.

Her heart melted a bit. He was so good to not only her, but her little dogs, too. She took his hands in hers. "I promise to think about this tomorrow. I'll even come up with a list of every man who's so much as looked at me in the past six months. But right now, for tonight, I need to forget. Think you can help me with that?"

"I have an idea or two," Jonah replied with a wink.

Chapter Six

Addie crept along the darkened hallway, aware that danger lurked within the shadows. She didn't know what form the danger would take or from which direction it would come, but the tiny hairs on the back of her neck stood at attention. Faint light spilled from the last room at the end of the hallway. She flattened back against the wall when she reached the room and peeked inside. A figure dressed in scrubs leaned over the bed. The weak light from a bedside lamp shone on the needle in the person's hand. She couldn't tell if it was a male or female.

"Just another moment, my dear, and you won't suffer anymore," the person whispered.

Addie gasped with horror, remembering when it was too late to cover her mouth.

The figure turned. "You!"

She jerked awake, then screamed at the sight of Grey lounging in her office doorway.

"You scared me," she accused her best friend.

"The screeching gave that away." His face softened. "Did you have another nightmare? I came to bring you a mug of tea. You looked tired this morning."

She yawned and stretched, proving his words. "I am, thanks. Come in, please."

He arched one blond brow but did as she asked without question. "Something's up."

Addie's shoulders sagged at the fact that he didn't ask but stated it. "I have to tell you something, and I need you to promise you won't freak out."

"Good freak or bad freak?"

She barked out a laugh. Grey was always good for a laugh, even in the worst of times. "Sadly, a bad one."

"Oh." He moved to the edge of his chair. "Either way, I'm here for you. Always."

"And you know I love you for it."

She took a deep breath and expelled it slowly before telling him about the note on her door last evening. She had to give him credit, he sat and listened through the whole sordid tale. Not once did he interrupt. But his very expressive face spoke volumes. She took a sip of tea to fortify herself. She knew what was coming.

"Is that all? Are you done now?"

Addie nodded.

"What the hell, Addie? Why didn't you tell me last night?" He jumped out of his chair and paced her small office. "This has to stop. When I get my hands on this cretin…"

"Remember the part about *not* freaking out?"

"That was before you told me you'd been threatened." He looked at her set face. "Fine." He sat back down. In a softer, more controlled tone, he added, "What's the next step?"

"I'm so glad you asked, because I need help with this part." She told him about Jonah asking her for the names of people she'd had any kind of run in with. "To review, we don't think it's Noah or anyone I know very well. And it's probably not anyone who lives here in Ocean Grove. Or at least didn't live here a long time. He could be new to town or someone who has a reason to be here regularly."

"Leaving us the rest of the male population of North Carolina and beyond? Great!"

"We'll leave that part up to the police. We have to come up with a list of names."

"So Deputy Do-Wrong is finally taking this seriously?"

Addie tried to keep a straight face at his less-than-flattering nickname for Jonah's partner, Dan Blackwell. "Now, Grey, play nice."

Grey snorted. "You don't like him either. Not sure Jonah even likes him."

"I believe Jonah, uh, respects him." She sighed. "I am not a fan. He tends to play down the things that happen."

"Like when he came out after the bear had been left? I seem to recall him finding it funny someone 'had the hots for you.' He's creepy."

She chose not to respond, as she'd always found him a bit creepy as well. "Everyone at the station, starting with the chief of police, is taking this seriously because there is an actual threat this time. And not just to me." Her breath hitched on the last part, and she sent a silent message out to the universe to keep Jonah safe.

"Well, whatever the reason, at least they're paying attention now. So, let's start on the list." He grabbed a scratch pad and a pen from the corner of her desk. "Are you sure we're not listing Noah?"

"I don't believe it's him. Nor does Jonah. But to be safe, and inclusive, go ahead and write his name down."

Grey, who'd never been a huge Noah fan, did just that, putting him at the top of the list. He followed it up with several more.

She turned the paper around to get a better look. "Who's Caden? And Mr. Mc Manus? How did he make the list?"

"Caden is the barista next door. He moved here a few months ago. And why not Mr. Mc Manus? Everyone knows he's the meanest person in Ocean Grove."

"You're not wrong about Mr. Mc Manus. But being mean doesn't put him on the short list of possible stalkers. And Caden is maybe twenty."

"You're point being, Mrs. Robinson?"

She stuck out her tongue at him. "Very funny, Grey."

Jonah's dark head popped into her office. He smiled at her before entering her already crowded office. "Hey, man," Jonah said to Grey before turning to Addie and kissing her. "Do you have the list?"

She motioned to the only other empty chair available. "We were just talking about that. As you can see, we haven't gotten very far." She pointed to the three names.

"I thought we ruled out Noah."

"We did. Putting him on the list made Grey feel better."

"I never like him," the man in question muttered.

"In your defense, neither did I. Dating a patient is just wrong."

"Former patient." She threw up her hands. "Why am I defending him?"

"Good question." Jonah looked at the list again. "Isn't Mr. Mc Manus almost eighty? Although he might be the meanest guy in town, I think we're safe to cross him off."

"See? I was right," Addie crowed to her friend.

"How do you know about him?" asked Grey.

Jonah shook his head. "Everyone in law enforcement in Ocean Grove knows him. That man comes in at least once a week to lodge a complaint about something or someone. If it's not his neighbor's dog barking, then it's someone who dared to jaywalk in town. That man is a menace but not your stalker."

"Agreed," said Addie.

"And who is Caleb?"

She laughed. "You can take him off, too. He's about twenty and a part-time barista at Wide Awake Cafe next door."

"Age doesn't rule him out, Addie."

"And there's the way he looks at you. Don't forget to tell Jonah that," added Grey with a bit of mischief sparkling in his blue eyes.

"Oh, and how does he look at you, Addie?" Jonah asked, one eyebrow cocking.

"Again, he's twenty!"

"Like he likes her. You know, likes her, likes her," Grey added by way of explanation.

"That's enough out of you. And I would kick you out of my office, but I had another dream I have to tell you both about."

Both men turned to face her. "Just now, before Grey woke me up. I guess I fell asleep."

"We didn't get a lot of sleep last night," murmured Jonah

"Really? Do tell!" commented Grey.

Addie ignored the heat seeping into her face. The thought of why she'd lost sleep made her smile. "Anyway, it was very similar to the last one, but different." She laughed at the confusion written on both men's faces. "Sorry, that wasn't very clear."

"About as clear as mud, as my dear, departed granny would say."

"You're right, Grey. The dream was the same in that it happened in the same creepy, dark hallway. The setting was definitely the same. But it differed, because somehow, I knew to be careful. I crept down the hallway, not wanting to alert someone to my presence. Weird, right?"

"Very," agreed Jonah. "Go on. What else happened?"

"I had my back to the wall and peeked around the doorway to see what was happening. Someone stood over a bed, with a needle in their hand. They whispered to the person in the bed in a quiet, almost soothing, voice."

"Almost? Why wasn't it?"

"I'm not sure. There was something about the voice…something off. Or maybe it had to do with the needle in their hand." She shuddered remembering the rest of the dream. "And then I gasped, and the person turned to look at me. Caught me there."

"You keep saying 'their' and 'someone' without using he or she. Do you not know? Try to remember," Jonah urged her.

Addie closed her eyes, trying to recall the details of the dream. "The room was mostly dark, draped in shadows, with only a dim light coming from the bedside lamp. The person wore scrubs that were baggy and didn't reveal a shape per se. It could have been a she or a smaller man. The figure was slight." She opened her eyes and stared at the men in front of her, relieved by their presence as she tried to shake off the threat of the vision. "There was something very scary about the person."

Jonah covered her cold hands with his own. "I'm guessing the needle wasn't a normal part of care. Maybe something ordered for the patient?"

"I don't believe so. There was a furtiveness about him. Or her." She squeezed his hands in thanks for his support. Honestly, she had no idea why he hadn't run for the hills yet with all this craziness. "I figured you should both know."

"Of course we should. Maybe Granny Betsy needs a bed there sooner than we thought. Maybe we should go back again, have another look around."

"No." Jonah turned his head and fixed Grey with a stare. "You two are done cavorting around. I'll look into this."

"Geez, take away my fun, why don't you. You're just miffed because Addie and I were married."

"That's the least of my worries," Jonah mumbled.

"Boys! Maybe we can concentrate on the task, or tasks, at hand. Jonah, I promise not to go back there. At least not without you. And I'll put any names I can think of on the list. And Grey,

you will behave yourself."
"Ah, what fun is that?"

Chapter Seven

The rest of Addie's Sunday passed without incident. Sales had picked up with Christmas less than a month away. She put the name of every male she'd interacted with, and could remember, on the list for Jonah. None of them seemed a likely candidate for her stalker, but you never knew.

Before Jonah went back to the station, they'd made plans for an early dinner. Although they both enjoyed last night's 'stress relief,' they'd decided actual sleep was called for tonight. Jonah planned to be at her house by seven, with takeout from wherever he picked. This upcoming week would be very busy, between the store and the holiday. The next few weeks until Christmas always proved to be the busiest of the year. And while she wasn't complaining, she had a lot of work ahead of her.

Her minuscule stockroom already overflowed with new inventory.

After the last customer left, Addie switched the sign to 'Sea you tomorrow' and locked the front door. Living near the beach gave her the opportunity for all kinds of fun nautical expressions. Although being in the store alone after the note creeped her out more than a little, she had work to do. Those shelves weren't going to stock themselves. The fact that she was locked in helped. She walked around the store first, gathering books that had been pulled then discarded. She usually did this as the shop was closing, but the day's last-minute crush of customers hadn't left her any time. Not that she was complaining. When she'd scooped up all the strays, Addie headed into the backroom to grab the first few boxes.

She debated in her head between starting in the adult or children's section when the lights went out. Addie gripped the boxcutter in her hand until her fingers cramped. She stood very still, listening for anything that would indicate another person in the store with her. Although she was happy Grey had taken the girls to the Aunties, they made an excellent early warning system. She held her breath, afraid even that slight noise would give away her location. Although she'd been sure she was alone when she locked up, she didn't feel very confident about it now.

No noise came from the outer room. She

strained to hear, but it would be hard to hear anything faint over the rushing of her pulse in her own ears. She gripped the boxcutter with one hand and slid her phone out of her back pocket with the other. After ducking behind a tall stack of boxes, Addie slid her finger across the screen to unlock it before hitting Jonah's preset. It rang a few times before his voicemail clicked on.

Damn!

She waited until the beep, ridiculously loud in the dark room, before whispering into the phone. "Jonah, it's me. Something's wrong at the store. The lights went out. Please hurry. I'm calling nine-one-one." She hung up the phone and did just that.

"Nine-one-one, what's your emergency?"

"I think someone is trying to break in," Addie whispered into the phone, afraid to make any noise.

"Ma'am, are you okay? I can barely hear you," the female dispatcher stated.

Sweat trickled down Addie's neck as she crouched lower behind the boxes. "Someone left a threatening note at my home yesterday, and now the lights have gone off in my store. I'm here alone. Can you s-s-send help, please?" She rattled off the name and address just in case the dispatcher needed them.

"Okay, ma'am, tell me your name."

"Addie Foster."

"All right, Addie, my name is Stephanie,

and I'm going to stay with you. I have police on their way. Where are you in the store, Addie?"

"I'm in the back storeroom, hiding behind a stack of boxes. I don't think they can see me."

"They? Is there more than one person involved?"

She shook her head before remembering the dispatcher couldn't see her. "I don't know. I didn't actually see, or hear, anyone."

"Are you armed, Addie? I have to tell my officers."

A giggle escaped her pressed lips. "I have a boxcutter. I don't believe in guns. At least I never did. Now, I wish I had one."

"That doesn't always end the way people think it would. Do me a favor, take some deep breaths for me, and stay on the line."

Addie did, and it made her feel a little better. But her legs ached from holding her crouching position. She longed to stand or sit but remained frozen to the spot. "Stephanie, I don't hear anything. But I'm too scared to move."

"Stay exactly where you are. I don't want you to go out there."

She stifled a nervous laugh. "Don't worry, I won't."

"Good. My first officer is right around the corner from your position. His name is Mike Bradley. Is there a back entrance to the store?"

Relief washed over Addie at the familiar name. He was the officer who'd been injured protecting her last summer. "The back door is maybe twenty feet from where I am. It's locked. The front is locked as well."

"When I tell you to, can you reach the back door to open it without putting yourself at risk?" Stephanie asked.

The thought of moving from her position sent a flood of icy sweat down her back. But she'd feel safer once an officer arrived. "Y-y-yes, I can do that." She crossed her fingers, hoping she could. Even two minutes seemed like a very long time right about now. "Can you reach Jonah, uh, I mean Detective Wolfe? I called him first, but he didn't answer."

"Yes, ma'am, I'll have someone do that. Officer Bradley should be there any second. I just need you to hang on for a little while longer."

"Thank you for staying on the line with me. I don't feel so scared."

But she'd spoken too soon. The sound of the front door rattling almost stopped her heart. "Someone's trying to get in the front door. Please have him hurry."

"He should be on scene right now, ma'am. Do me a favor and move to the door."

Addie crept toward the backdoor, her legs burning with the effort after crouching for so long. She picked her way behind rows of boxes, desperate to remain hidden, but the boxes ended halfway to the door. Knowing she had to risk it, Addie sucked in a deep breath and ran the rest of the way, collapsing against the door. "Officer Bradley is that you?" she whispered against the metal.

"Ms. Foster, it's me. Can you let me in?" came a masculine voice.

His soothingly familiar voice set her in action. With shaking hands, she unlocked the back door, opening it only enough to allow him to squeeze in. "Oh, thank goodness," she whispered as she hugged him. "Thank you for coming. I don't know if anyone is up front or not."

"My pleasure, ma'am. There are two cars out front, checking the street. Should just be a moment now."

She let go of him and moved back behind the row of boxes as the radio clipped to his jacket squawked to life. Addie couldn't make out what was being said, but she hoped it was good news.

"Ms. Foster, everything is clear up there. I'm going to go open the door and let in the other officers. Will you be okay alone for a moment?"

She gave him a wan smile and nodded.

He reached behind himself and locked the back door. "Give me a minute. I'll let you know when it's clear to come out."

Relief flooded through her, and she sat down hard on the ground as her knees gave out. Now that she was safe, she found it hard to breathe. She rubbed at the ache in her chest.

Addie stayed in that position. She heard him rush up front, followed by the sound of the door opening. A few different voices all seemed to speak at once, but only one caught her attention.

"Where is she?" came Jonah's distinctive baritone.

"I'm back here," she cried. She couldn't even get off the floor before he reached her, gathering her in his arms and lifting her up.

"Addie, I was so worried," he whispered into her hair.

She clung to him to him like a drowning person to a life preserver. "Thank you for coming. I was so scared."

"I'm so sorry I didn't answer. I had stopped in to grab our dinner and left my phone in the car. Never again, I promise." He hugged her so hard she could barely breathe, but nothing had ever felt better. Or safer.

"You have nothing to apologize for. How could you have known?"

"Well, now I know." Jonah kissed the top of her head. "Nothing is more precious to me than you."

"Right back at you," she managed past the lump in her throat. If she told him how she really felt, how very important he'd become to her, she'd lose it. Tears everywhere. She sniffed and pulled away from him. "I need to see what's happening." She ignored the confusion in his eyes and walked out of the storeroom.

Three cops moved about her store,

checking the door and windows. "Can anyone tell me what happened?"

Officer Bradley turned toward her. "Looks like the power was cut at the box outside. Should be easy enough to fix once we're done."

"Done?"

"Oh, done with investigating." The younger man straightened to his full height in front of her. "We've got this, Ms. Foster. We'll find out who did this and why."

Addie held in a snicker. Jonah had once mentioned he thought the patrol officer had a little crush on her. Of course, he growled when he said it. Seemed he was right. Then she remembered the stalker and how it could be anyone.

"I've got this, Mike," Jonah announced coming to stand next to her. He placed an arm around Addie, tugging her against him. Normally that kind of pissing match irritated her, but Officer Bradley nodded and left the building. She'd take it.

"Who would do this? And why? Was he just trying to scare me? Or was he planning something else?" The endless, unpleasant scenarios whirled in her head.

Jonah turned to her. "We have to assume this is tied in with the 'gifts' you've received. Whoever it is has stepped up his game, become more threatening. No more taking any chances, Addie."

"What chances have I taken? I stayed in the store all day, even letting Grey go for lunch because God forbid, I walk two blocks in broad daylight. I was locked in my own store, all safe and sound. What else could I have done?"

"That's just it, Addie. You were locked in your own store, alone, and this happened." He threw up his hands. "You cannot be alone anymore. Anywhere. We can't take the chance. What if he had busted in, not just terrified you? What if I'd gotten here too late?"

Jonah's voice drifted to just above a whisper by the end. Addie's heart squeezed in her chest. What was she doing to him? "I get it, Jonah. I do. But I can't live like this. And I really can't ask you to either." She started to walk away; hot tears threatened again, but for a different reason this time.

He grabbed her wrist. "Oh, no you don't, Adelaide Foster. You're not getting away from me that easily. I'm in this for the long haul, crazy stalker and all."

"I can't ask you to do that, Jonah." She looked into his dark eyes, seeing love all mixed up with fear and something she couldn't identify.

"You never asked me to. Remember? I'm here, in this mess with you, because there's nowhere I'd rather be."

And in that moment, she knew he was telling the truth. Being Jonah. She threw her arms around his waist, burying her face in his chest. "I'm probably going to fall apart a little later. When we're not standing here with all these people. I'm going to cry until you think I'll never stop. But you'll be right there with me, even though women crying makes you very uncomfortable. And I'll love you even more for doing it, although I don't know how that's even possible."

"Yes to all that, Addie, and so much more. One day, there won't be a crazed stalker after you. There might even be a period of time when you don't have prophetic, scary dreams and someone isn't trying to kill one or both of us. But even if that's not true, I'm still going to be right here. With you."

She hugged him tighter for a moment before letting go. "Okay, then, sounds like a plan. I'd really like to go home. Can we wrap this up?"

"My thoughts exactly."

Chapter Eight

Addie got out of the bath only when the water made her teeth chatter. She dried off and threw on pajamas and her oldest, heaviest robe. It was the comfort food of clothing. About as sexy as a hospital gown, but she'd take it.

A delicious aroma teased her nose as she stepped into the kitchen. "I didn't hear you leave, and I don't own the ingredients for that kind of dinner." She smiled at Jonah. He'd removed his tie, unbuttoned a few buttons, and rolled up the sleeves of his dress shirt. Already, he looked less like Detective Wolfe and more like the man she loved.

He held up his phone. "No reason to leave when there's an app for that."

"Ah, Food 2 U, the delight of hungry but lazy people everywhere." She closed her eyes and sniffed. "Is that Angelo's I smell? Oh, I so hope that's Angelo's Penne a la Vodka."

Jonah walked up to her and tapped the end of her nose. "Good guess. I figured after what just happened, Angelo's Penne a la Vodka was the right choice."

"The only choice." She threw her arms around him. "You know me so well."

A chorus of excited yips sounded from the kitchen slider. "And the girls are home." Addie rushed to the kitchen door to let them in. They crowded her, competing for attention as if they'd been separated for days rather than hours. She pet their fluffy bodies, fur cool from the evening air. When she straightened, both dogs ran to the table, noses scenting the air. "Apparently, I'm not the only ones who can appreciate good food around here," she joked.

"Grey dropped them off a few minutes ago. I invited him to stay, but he had a hot date. His words, not mine."

Jonah whistled once, and both dogs ran to their bowls in the kitchen. She watched as he measured out their evening meal, talking to them and patting both as he went. He washed his hands at the sink before turning to her. "They aren't stupid. They know we're about to have some very yummy people food. We have maybe three minutes."

Addie laid out the food, opening containers and ripping off a chunk of crusty, Italian bread. "This seems so normal, despite everything that's happened." She dipped the chunk into the Vodka sauce and popped it in her mouth, sighing at the explosion of flavor.

"This is normal. Our normal. This is the choice we make. No matter what might be happening around us, this remains our normal. Having dinner together, even feeding the dogs. Spending time together. I've learned never to take anything for granted."

She thought about his father dying in front of him when Jonah was little, murdered at the hands of a drugged-out thief. She thought about losing her own mother way too young.

"You're right." Addie took a few bites of her food before setting down her fork. "I have a strange question for you."

Jonah looked at her, fork paused half-way to his mouth. "I'm almost afraid to ask, but go on." He ate the piece of Veal Piccata, chewing and swallowing while waiting for her to ask.

"Today, in the store, Mike…uh…Officer Bradley, acted a little…" She wasn't sure how to phrase it.

"A little like he has a huge crush on you? Is that what you were trying so hard to not say?"

She shifted in her seat. "Well, yeah."

"That's because he does." He took another bite.

"And you're okay with that? I mean, he's your coworker. And I'm your girlfriend."

"What can I say? He has good taste." Jonah easily caught the napkin she tossed at him. "Addie, listen. Mike is a good guy; good cop, even. And he's very young. Even if you and I weren't together, I don't think he'd be your type."

Addie shook her head. "He's very sweet, but he's way too young for me."

"Exactly. And you and I both know you don't get to choose who you have feelings for. Or fall in love with. If that were true, would I have fallen for a blood-soaked murder suspect?"

"True." They had a very odd beginning to their relationship; him finding her covered in blood but not her own. And then she fainted on him. "So, here's the thing. I wonder if the person who's stalking me is like that."

"You don't think it's Mike, I hope?"

"No, of course not. But what if it's some guy I was nice to, smiled at as he bought a book from my store? How do you know when your innocent gesture becomes fodder for someone's disturbed fantasy life?" She shuddered, thinking about all the people she interacted with daily. "It's not something I ever thought about."

"But now you have to."

"Yes." She smiled at the lack of a questioning tone in his voice. "Now, I have to think about every man I meet, or pass on the street. Is he looking at me oddly? Did he smile too much? Did I?"

Jonah set his fork down and took her hands in his. "No matter what happens, know this. You didn't do anything wrong. You didn't lead him on or tease him. You certainly didn't ask for this."

Addie blew out a pent-up breath. "I know that. Really, I do. But I needed to hear you say it. I don't want to change who I am or how I see the world. I don't want to be afraid every time I hand a customer change."

"Then don't. I know the words are easy. All I mean is don't let this change you. Then he really wins."

She squeezed his hand before pulling back hers. "Good. Because I don't want to become some person who's afraid of her own shadow. I want to live my life, meet people, enjoy the day."

"Then that's what you'll do. But right now, I need you to be careful."

"You, too, Mister. As we know, you're not bulletproof."

He winced at her choice of words. "Point taken. However, I'm usually armed."

"Got me there."

"Seriously, Addie, I want you to think about your actions. Don't stay alone in the store. Just for now, until we catch this guy." He looked so intently into her eyes, she believed he could see into her soul. "Please."

She made a little motion across her chest. "Cross my heart. But same goes for you. I know you're a tough guy and all, but I almost lost you once."

"Agreed."

They finished their evening the way most

couples do, eating dinner and then arguing over what to watch on TV. Addie soaked it in, the normalcy of it. For a few hours, she could pretend they were just that. A normal couple. She forgot about the terrifying, prophetic dreams and angry missives from a stranger. She reveled in snuggling on the couch with Jonah, while the girls lay at their feet.

They turned in early, gearing up for the holiday week, and making up for lost sleep last night. Addie kissed him goodnight and curled into the circle of his arms, then sent a silent message into the universe to keep the bad dreams at bay.

She stood flattened against the wall outside the room at the end of the hallway. Her breathing was labored, coming in pants and gasps. Addie covered her mouth; afraid she'd give away her location. It was the same room in the same hallway, familiar only from her nightmares. She gathered her courage and peeked around the doorway. The same person dressed in scrubs, stood next to the bed. Only this time, they were closer to the nightstand, not blocking the person in the bed from her view.

"No, I don't want to die," cried a feeble voice from the bed. Addie inched closer, straining to identify the familiar voice. And then Mrs. Henry raised her head from the pillow. "See, Addie, I told you they murdered Bill. Now it's too late for me."

"And for you," the person standing next to the bed muttered as they turned toward her.

Addie jolted awake, a sheen of perspiration coating her. She clutched her chest, willing her heart to slow its frantic tempo.

Jonah sat up, turning to her. He enclosed her shaking body in his arms. "Another one, I guess."

"Yes," she cried, telling him what she could remember as she sobbed. "It was Mrs. Henry lying in the bed. She said it was my fault because I hadn't believed her." She buried her head against his warm chest. The dreams had never been so real. She could hear the fear in the older woman's trembling voice. Felt the weight of her accusation.

"It's okay, honey. It was only a dream." Jonah swiveled and tapped his phone. "It's not quite four. Try to get some more sleep." He laid back down, pulling her stiff body with him.

Addie wanted to believe him, that everything was fine. But she knew better. "I have to know she's okay. I could call and check."

"I know you do, but it's four in the morning. And you aren't family. Even if you called right now, they're not going to tell you anything. Wait until morning. You can call and ask to speak with her then. Put your mind at ease."

She turned in his arms, laying her head on his chest. "I know you're right. And I'll wait until a decent time. But I have a very bad feeling that won't go away."

"I know you do." He trailed one hand

along her back in a soothing moment. "Let's talk about something else, try to take your mind off things. I know. Tell me more about what to expect for Thanksgiving dinner."

His soft laugh rumbled through his chest, vibrating against her cheek. She settled against him, happy once again for this lovely man. "Well, first there's the turkeys."

That caught his attention. "Did you say turkeys? As in plural?"

"I did indeed."

"Should I ask why?"

"Each aunt makes her own turkey. It's part of the Great Dressing Wars, as Grey and I call it."

"Interesting. Thanksgiving is funny to me. I get the being thankful and all, although I believe you should be thankful every day. But the food. Everyone gets so excited about the turkey, when really it's everything else I look forward to."

She squealed. "Me, too! I've always thought the turkey only serves as a centerpiece. It's the sides I love. And then, of course, there are the desserts."

Jonah smacked his lips in the dark. "I imagine Gertie will bring a pie or two."

"Well, of course. And then there's the other desserts."

"Other?"

"Yes, the great debate is not only about dressing. Every year, we discuss the various pros and cons of pie versus cake."

Jonah groaned. "There's going to be cake, too?"

Addie laughed at the sound of his voice; that of a little boy in a candy store. "Yes, Jonah, there will be at least one but more likely two."

"Dare I even hope for Clementine's Death by Chocolate cake?"

"I think that's a pretty safe bet."

"Oh good. That's my favorite cake ever. But don't tell Gertie. I wouldn't want to hurt her feelings."

She giggled, the horror of the dream receding with their banter. Just like she knew he wanted. "Well, hold your horses. You haven't tried Beatrice's Hummingbird Cake. I wouldn't announce a favorite until you have."

He raised up on one elbow, peering down into her face. "Are you kidding me? I haven't had one of those since my grandmother died. Took the recipe to her grave, much to my mother's horror."

"I never kid about dessert," she joked, poking him in the ribs with one finger. "I did mention you weren't ready for this meal."

She saw his expression change in the soft glow from the open curtain. He wagged his eyebrows. "Well, then. I'd better get in some conditioning."

Addie shrieked as he pounced on her, nibbling his way along her neck.

Addie waited until nine in the morning to call Magnolia Haven. She'd busied her mind with making a quick breakfast for them, then stopping for a pumpkin-spiced latte at Wide Awake Cafe next door to her bookstore. But now she couldn't wait any longer. Although Jonah had done his best to reassure, and distract her, she worried about her friend. Mrs. Henry reminded her very much of her Aunties; the word elderly didn't apply. The octogenarian had travelled the world until well into her seventies, when she lost her beloved husband. Addie enjoyed her stories about far-flung places. She and her husband, a civil engineer, had never had children. Made the decision to never have them; 'rug rats,' as Mrs. Henry referred to them. Instead, she chose to live a vagabond lifestyle, following her husband from one work assignment to the other.

Addie waited on hold, her tenuous patience fraying. She'd already spoken with two people, being passed along to whomever might be the right person. She glanced around the shop as she waited. Colorful decorations in all the lovely shades of fall, reds, greens, yellows, and browns, peeked out here and there. A very old, stuffed turkey, named Tom for obvious reasons, held court in the children's section. Tom had belonged to her mother from childhood. Her mother, a life-long vegetarian, liked to joke that Tom was the only turkey she needed. Tom looked a bit worn from years of tiny hands petting him, but Addie wouldn't have it any other way.

A voice finally picked up, and Addie jumped right in with her inquiry.

"Hello, I'm hoping you can help me. I'm calling to ask about my friend, Mrs. Henry, who lives in your facility. I don't have her private phone number and was wondering if you could connect me."

"I'm so sorry, but we aren't allowed to give out information on our residents. Surely, there's family you could contact."

"Well, no, actually there isn't any family. At least none I'm aware of. That's why I'm asking you. She comes into my bookstore quite regularly, and I haven't seen her in a while. I wanted to see that she's okay." She crossed her fingers at the small lie. Desperate times calling for desperate measures and all that.

"I am sorry, ma'am, but I can't help you. We have very strict rules about privacy here. Have a good day," the voice ended on a falsely cheery note before disconnecting the call.

"Rats," Addie muttered to the empty store.

As she tapped her fingers on the countertop, trying to come up with a plan B, brisk knocking at the locked front door caught her attention. Normally she'd rush over to answer, but having an unknown stalker had changed that habit. Gracey and Lily barked from their shared bed at her feet. The lack of a throaty growl gave her some courage. Addie sidled along the length of the counter, peeking toward the front door as she went.

"Oh, for Pete's sake, Adelaide Foster, we're not getting any younger out here."

"Give the girl a chance, Clementine," commanded Aunt Beatrice.

Almost weak with relief, Addie hurried to the door to let them in. "What are you two doing out and about so early on a Monday morning?" She stood back and let her aunts pass into the store.

"We have our hair appointments in a bit. Thought we'd stop by see how you're doing. It's not like you ever come to see us anymore," groused Clementine.

Addie hurried to each one, giving them a peck on the cheek. In all the confusion of the past few days, she'd never gotten around to checking in on them. Hardly a day went by without a phone call or inappropriate text. The latter usually had something to do with her aging eggs.

"I'm so sorry. It's been a bit hectic, what with the holiday and all coming." She chose to leave out recent events, not wanting to alarm them more than necessary. Best to mention her stalker once he was caught and no longer posed a threat.

Beatrice stepped forward and patted Addie on the arm. "So no more threats, then?"

Addie felt her jaw scrape the floor and

couldn't do anything to stop it. "How did you know about that?" She then saw the gleam in Clementine's eye and shook her head. "Ah, let me guess. Blond, over six feet tall, can't keep a secret to save his life?"

"Now, Adelaide, there's no point in blaming dear Greyson. At least he cares enough to tell us the truth."

They only called her "Adelaide" when she was in trouble, so Addie bit back a retort. "You know I love both of you more than Heaven and Earth combined. I was trying to protect y'all. Keep you from worrying." She thought about choking her best friend but knew it wouldn't come to violence. Grey loved her like the sister he never had. And besides, life without him would be boring.

Her text alert buzzed. "Excuse me one second, please." She pulled her phone from her back pocket, glancing at the screen. *Call me,* sent by Jonah less than a minute ago.

She held up a finger for her aunts and hit his preset. He answered on the first ring.

"Should I sit down?" she asked, holding her breath.

"It's not great news. I'm sorry but Mrs. Henry is in the hospital. Apparently, she fell and broke her arm. Or maybe her ankle."

Addie sat down on the first surface she could find. "How did you find out?"

"Well, I knew you'd worry, so I called around. She was admitted to Ocean Grove

Memorial late Saturday night. The good news is, she's being released today. That's all I know."

Addie sucked in a breath. "Are we sure that's good news? What if she's next? What if my dream is right?" She heard the gasps from her Aunties. In her concern for Mrs. Henry, she'd forgotten they were there. Nothing she could do now. "I want to go see her, but I'm not sure if that's the best thing after what Grey and I did on Saturday."

"You may be right about that. Let me think about it. I have to go. Talk later?"

"Yes, of course. And thank you. I love you."

"I love you, too, Addie. See you later." He disconnected the call.

She turned to face the Aunties. "I'm not sure how much of that you heard," she started, then stopped at the determined looks on their faces.

"Say no more," advised Beatrice.

"We're on it," finished Clementine.

"Hold it right there. Please. I can't have either of you getting involved in this...well, I'm not sure what it is, but you know what I mean."

Clementine pulled herself to her full height, not at all intimidating at just over five feet tall. Addie didn't have the heart to break the news. "We're just two concerned old ladies going to visit an injured friend." She winked at Addie, blowing her cover.

Before Addie could try to talk them out of

this hair-brained idea, the two turned and marched toward the door. Beatrice turned as she left, stating, "If he loves you so much, when's he gonna put a ring on it?"

Addie just stood there, befuddled as usual after dealing with the Aunties, and watched them go.

Chapter Nine

Hours later, Addie looked up from her phone when she felt the weight of a stare. Grey, in all his glory, leaned against the other side of the counter. She sighed and closed her Kindle app. One great irony of owning a bookstore, and being surrounded by books every day, is that she rarely had time to read. "Yes? How may I help you?"

Not in the least bit put off by her tone for interrupting the first quiet five-minute period they'd had that day, he merely grinned at her. "I was trying to picture Beatrice quoting Beyoncé."

"Oh. It looked pretty much like how I'm sure you're imagining it. And please don't encourage that. The last thing Jonah needs is the Aunties pressuring him to propose. It's only been a few short weeks."

"True enough I suppose, but neither of you is getting any younger." Grey laughed at his own quip, something he did a lot. "Oh, I know. I could mention our baby pact again. He wasn't thrilled with that."

Addie groaned while shaking her head. "Please don't." When they were nineteen and drunk one night in college, Addie and Grey made a bizarre pact to have a baby together if they reached a certain (and still undefined) age without either having married. Having been friends since longer than either of them could really remember, not to mention his being gay, was what made it bizarre. Grey, being Grey, had mentioned it to Jonah very early on. Long before they were together. Because of his growing, and hidden at the time feelings for her, it had gone over like a fart in church.

"You're no fun. With the latest round of terrifying dreams, not to mention some madman wanting you and Jonah dead, I'd think you'd be up for some type of fun." He pulled one of his legendary pouts. The one that worked on everyone, except her.

Addie turned as the bell over the door chimed, announcing a customer. "Nice try. I'm not going to be a part of your little scenario to poke the bear."

"Let me guess, I'm the bear." Jonah entered and strode over to the desk, leaning over to kiss her on the lips. He then turned to Grey. "What trouble are you up to now?"

A warmth spread in her chest at his words. Although his voice held a rough note, it was laced with his obvious fondness for her best friend. The two very different men had become great friends because they shared one very important thing in common. Her.

"Oh, nothing," murmured Grey.

"Nothing worth mentioning is what he meant to say," she answered. "What brings you here in the middle of your busy detective day?"

He held up a take-out bag. "I thought I'd bring lunch. Steal a few minutes with my best girl."

"Better be only girl," Grey sniped with a raised brow.

"Goes without saying. Keep that up, and I won't hand over your fortune cookie, Grey."

She laughed at Grey's crestfallen look. Her friend was a sucker for a good fortune cookie fortune. The ones he liked, he carried around in his wallet until they came true, thus 'proving' them. This was just one of a million quirky things she loved about him.

"Fine, I'll be good! Now hand it over." Grey held out his hand, palm up, and waited.

Jonah held in a laugh as he handed over one of the individually wrapped cookies. "You're worse than a toddler."

"No, I'm not. My hands are never sticky." He shuddered. Grey's view of the children who came in the store were well known to all.

Jonah shook his head and took their lunch from the shopping bag. "Shrimp lo mein for the lady. Szechuan Chicken for Grey." He passed a container to each of them. "Chicken and cashews for me."

They found seats in the reading area, spreading out their lunches on the low table.

"Spicy, like me," Grey joked before opening his lunch.

Jonah rolled his eyes. "What were you guys discussing when I came in?"

Addie counted to ten in her head, not wanting to bring it up.

"She and I having a baby," Grey announced around a mouthful of fortune cookie. Because he always ate that first. Life was short.

"Why? She has me for that, now."

She had to give Jonah credit. He didn't miss a beat. And he knew how to shut Grey up, a skill few possessed. Still, her heart beat a funny little rhythm in her chest at the thought.

"He was being difficult, as always. And he was kidding. Weren't you, Grey?"

"Yes, of course I was. And if by chance I wasn't, don't worry. We'd be using one of those turkey basters." He wrinkled his nose, as if thinking about how conception would happen without one.

"I see," muttered Jonah, although his tone said otherwise. "For the record, I'm not in the least bit threatened. I'm more curious as to why we're having this discussion. Again."

Addie tried hard not to choke on her noodles. Back when they'd first met, Grey tortured Jonah a bit, making it sound as though their "contingency plan" was a real thing about to happen. She grabbed her water bottle and took a swig. "It was nothing. Just Grey being Grey."

The man in question pointed a plastic fork at her. "Actually, as you know, it was the Aunties who brought up the whole marriage and babies thing." He swung the fork between her and Jonah. "Apparently, you're not getting any younger. Who is?"

One day, she really would kill him. She smiled brightly, mostly teeth for Grey's sake. "In their defense, and to take away any pressure you might feel, Jonah, they've been commenting on my eggs since way before you came into the picture." She felt her face burn, but she couldn't do anything about it.

"Oh, well, that makes sense." Jonah resumed eating, without further comment, leaving a dumbfounded Addie to stare at him.

"Anyway, now that they have a mission, the Aunties should be out of your hair, or ovaries, for a bit, Addie."

And that caught Jonah's attention. "Mission?" He looked from one to the other before sighing. "I'm not going to like this, am I?"

"Nope," smirked Grey.

"Let me explain." That was as far as Addie got. How to explain her aunts? Grey leaning forward in anticipation didn't help. "It's not as bad as it'll sound," she started weakly. "They were in the shop when you called and overheard about Mrs. Henry being in the hospital." She stopped at the darkening of Jonah's expression.

"Let me guess. They wanted to 'help.'" He set down his fork and wiped his mouth on a paper napkin. To Addie, it looked as though he was gathering patience.

"In my defense, short of tying them in a chair, I couldn't really stop them."

"I know. But it's enough to worry about your safety without adding them to the list."

"Ah, he's a keeper," crooned Grey.

"Shush, you." Even though he wasn't wrong. She turned to Jonah. "All they were going to do was go visit Mrs. Henry. See how she is. What harm could come from that?" She hoped her words held true.

"Let me see if I have this straight. First, you two go off posing as a married couple to 'investigate' Magnolia Haven. Now, your aunts, who have watched way too many crime-shows, are 'checking up on' Mrs. Henry. Have I missed anything?"

"No, that about sums it up," said Grey with a smirk, not at all put off by Jonah's glare.

"Y'all do remember what I do for a living, right? That I'm an actual detective?"

"Jonah, I really couldn't stop them. I did try." Addie twisted her hands in her lap. She loved her aunts, but sometimes they were a bit of a handful.

"She did," added Grey around a

mouthful of his lunch. He grabbed a bottled water and downed a quarter of it. "Whew! They sure know how to spice up a chicken." He wiped at tiny beads of sweat gathering on his forehead.

Jonah turned to her, a soft smile on his face. "Honey, I've met your aunts. Hell, they've interrogated me on my choice of underwear. You couldn't have stopped them. I just don't want anything to happen."

Her heart did that funny little flip thing it did around him. "I know. Neither do I. On a different note, anything come up with the letter left on my door?" The thought of some nameless, faceless someone threatening him, because of her, made her stomach flip in a different way altogether.

Jonah placed his hands over hers, lending silent support. "Nothing so far. Whoever he, or she, is, they at least know enough not to leave prints. Or saliva." He gripped her hand before resuming his lunch.

Addie did the same, thinking about every male she'd had even the slightest encounter with over the past few months. It was too much. Ocean Grove might be a small town, but she far from knew everyone. And then there was the constant influx of tourists. She squeezed her eyes shut in the midst of the wave of despair pouring over her.

She felt a hand on her arm and opened her eyes. Grey's grim face told her everything she needed to know. "It's okay," she told him.

"No, it's not. Some person thinks it's okay to screw with my best friend's life. Nothing okay about that," he muttered.

"Damn straight," Jonah agreed. A fierce grin then split his face. "But think how much fun it'll be when we catch the bastard."

Addie looked back and forth between these two very different men, wondering how she was so lucky to have both of them in her life.

She blew out a breath and said, "I don't know how to figure this out. Who could it be? Where do I start? How do I narrow it down?"

"It starts with logic," Jonah started. "Think about the time you started getting these 'gifts' for lack of a better word. He would have noticed you sometime before that."

"The flowers," she muttered, her feelings on that evidenced in her tone.

"Oh, right, the funeral bouquet," said Grey, his blue eyes dancing with mischief.

"Yes, the ones you somehow thought were from me. As if I'd ever buy you those." Jonah grimaced. "But at least we have a starting point. So, before Halloween."

"Going by what you suggested, I would have met him in the weeks before that."

"Or days even. You never know how long it took for him to focus on you."

She shuddered at the thought, the room suddenly feeling cooler. "Then maybe from the summer forward until I got those?"

Jonah nodded. "That time frame makes

sense. And it goes back far enough that we don't accidentally leave someone off the list."

Addie rose from her seat and crossed to the desk, reaching for a pen and paper. "How many people could I have possibly brushed by in that amount of time?" she asked with a hint of snark. She sat back down and chewed on her bottom lip while she thought.

"Start with anyone who sticks out," Jonah suggested. "Someone who made you think twice about the encounter."

"People who make you go, 'Hmmm?'" Grey joked.

"Very funny. But I get what you mean." Addie closed her eyes and tried to picture the past few months like a video playing in her mind. Who stood out? Nothing jumped out at her. She shook her head. "I'm sorry. I just don't know." She ground her teeth, desperate to come up with something that would help.

Grey got a look on his face. The one he made when he was right about something. "You have to put Caden on there. You know he has a huge crush on you. Gives you extra whipped cream in your hot chocolate."

"We talked about him, remember? He's a puppy."

Jonah slid the paper toward himself, grabbed the pen from Addie's hand and wrote the name. "I told you, age doesn't rule him out. Now, who else?"

Grey grabbed the paper next and

scrawled "Noah" in big, bold letters before sliding it back to her. She grimaced but nodded.

"Yes, he has to be on here I guess." She chewed on the pen, a memory niggling at the back of her brain. "Remember that guy in the bar, Grey? Near the beginning of the summer."

Grey's brows drew together as though in deep thought. Then his mouth formed a perfect O. "Teeth bleaching guy! Of course. How could I forget him?"

Jonah looked at each of them. "Teeth bleaching guy? I'm going to need more than that. Explain, please."

"I don't know his name. We saw him in the bar a couple times at the beginning of the summer. Wouldn't take no for an answer." She wrinkled her nose at the memory. "Much too handsy for me." She suppressed a grin as she watched Jonah's face go from curious to pissed in a heartbeat.

"What does that mean?" Jonah all but growled from between clenched teeth.

"Grey and I went for margaritas after closing one night over at The Tipsy Seagull on Ocean Way. And this guy stared at us for a while across the bar."

"Like, way too long to be comfortable," added Grey.

Addie grimaced before saying, "We joked about which of us might be the object of his affection."

"Turns out he was staring at her. And of

course Addie, who never thinks she's hot, acted totally oblivious to the whole thing. Which only made him stare more."

"In my defense, his stare wasn't one of interest. More of hunter to prey. It really creeped me out." She shuddered, remembering the feeling she got from his stare.

"And then he came over," drawled Grey in his manner.

"This is worse than watching paint dry. Tell me what happened," Jonah prompted.

"He started out sitting across the bar from us. And I did notice his intent stare. I chose to ignore it. And then suddenly it stopped."

"Because he was standing right next to you," added Grey.

Addie nodded. "I felt a hand on my shoulder, and when I turned, there he stood. Grinning. And he had the brightest teeth I'd ever seen."

Jonah grinned. "That explains the lovely nickname."

"Exactly," piped up Grey.

"But it was his eyes that got me." Addie shivered, remembering the dead, black look in them.

"What about his eyes?" Jonah asked.

"They were dead, flat, without any sign of life in them. And he pulled up the bar stool next to me, throwing an arm around my shoulder. I didn't like it."

"So, I stepped in." Grey puffed out his

chest. "Let him know she wasn't available."

"There was a moment where I wasn't sure he'd take the hint. Finally, he got up and left. But not before whispering, 'Not for long' in my ear as he left."

Chapter Ten

"Even though we don't have a name, he definitely goes on the list," Jonah snarled, scribbling on the paper.

Addie leaned forward, watching Jonah write 'creepy guy at bar' on the paper. "Well, that's progress. We have a twenty-year-old barista, one ex-barely even a boyfriend, and a stranger without a name. Any other thoughts?"

Jonah glanced at his phone. "I've gotta get back to the station." He stood, leaning down to kiss the top of Addie's head. "Keep at it. Anyone that gives you any pause at all belongs on the list." Turning to Grey, he added, "Don't let this one out of your sight. No matter what. See you later." He gathered his trash and headed out of the store.

"Stop watching his butt," Grey joked.

Addie didn't even try to hide her grin. "I

could say the same to you."

"You could."

The theme from The Golden Girls sang from her phone, announcing an incoming text from her aunts. Another of Grey's doings. She swiped a finger across the screen to read it, and muffled a gasp.

Mrs. H back at that place. Going 2 check it out.

Several emojis, including a gasping face, then a wink, followed the short missive. Addie slapped a hand over her mouth and groaned.

"Oh, this can't be good," she said, holding up the phone for Grey to read it also.

"Go, Aunties!" he exclaimed.

"Grey! The last thing those two need is encouragement." She buried her face in her hands and tried to think of a good way out of this mess. "What if something happens to them at Magnolia Haven? What if whoever the killer is notices them sniffing around Mrs. Henry?"

Grey's warm hands covered her chilly ones. "What if you take a deep breath? What if we think this through prior to panicking?" He whipped out his phone, fingers flying over the keyboard. "There. I sent a quick note to lover boy updating him. He'll know what to do. If anything needs to be done. Maybe, just maybe, Beatrice and Clementine will go to Murder Haven to visit a sick friend. Maybe no one will think anything else of it."

Addie tried to suppress a giggle without

much success. "You know very well, Grey, that the name is Magnolia Haven."

Grey's eyes crinkled as a huge smile wreathed his face. "But it made you laugh."

Addie rolled her head on her shoulders. "You're right, of course." She pointed one finger in his face. "Don't let that go to your head either."

"Never," he joked while he made a sign of crossing his heart. "You were saying something about me being right? Please, continue."

"There's no reason to panic just yet. The Aunties will go visit their ailing friend. Totally innocent." She held up crossed fingers. "Hopefully, they'll know to play it cool. Jonah will do his thing, figure out what needs to be done." She glanced down at the three names on the otherwise blank paper. "Remember the good old days, when I only had to worry about one person trying to k-k-kill m-m-me?" The last words came out with a wobble.

"This is a bit more, uh, challenging. I grant you that. But it'll be fine."

Addie raised her eyes to him, desperate to believe him. "How do you know?"

"Because it has to be."

*****

Closing time approached as Addie wandered around the store, replacing stray books on their appropriate shelves. A few customers lingered, wandering through the store. Grey's words echoed in her mind throughout the day. *Because it has to be.* She held onto the thought, repeating it to herself on and off. Addie generally thought of herself as a positive person. She'd dreamed of owning an independent bookstore, and here she was standing in the middle of it. Like all little girls, she'd dreamt of true love, and Jonah had come along. And although it was early days still, it didn't feel like it.

As though she had conjured him, the bells tinkled over the door, and in strode Jonah. She rushed to him, throwing her arms around him and inhaling the crisp, autumn air he brought in with him. She buried her nose in his chest, inhaling deeper to catch the innate male scent of him, something spicy and uniquely him.

"I missed you, too," he growled into the top of her head. His strong arms tightened around her, binding her to him.

The words rumbled through his chest, tickling her. Reassuring her. Jonah had become her rock in the storm of madness swirling around her at times. She reached up, kissing his throat before pulling away. "It's been a day."

"Good day, I hope."

"Great day for the store. You gotta love Christmas shoppers."

"And for you?"

She held out a hand, tilting it back and

forth. "It's hard to know what to worry about most, what's happening at Magnolia Haven or who wants to hurt us."

"That's some toss-up. Maybe flip a coin?"

"That seems like more of a Grey comment."

"I resemble that remark," quipped Grey as he joined them from the storage room. "Other than moi, what are we discussing?"

"Which of the troubling issues in my life to address first. Care to weigh in?" An older man standing at the counter caught her attention. "Let me take care of him and close up before we have this discussion."

Addie moved off to do just that, wincing at the overly loud sounds of both aunts entering the store. She rang up her customer's purchases, walked him to the door and flipped the "Closed" sign. She took a deep breath and squared her shoulders before joining the small crowd gathered in the seating area. The Aunties, as always, held court.

"Oh the poor dear, bless her heart, looked so old lying in that bed!" Clementine held a hand to her own heart, her face exuding sympathy.

Addie bit her lip. "What did I miss?"

Jonah stood, offering her his seat. "Your aunts were filling us in on Mrs. Henry."

She sat in his vacated chair, comforted by the weight of his hand on her shoulder. "How is she? Is she in much pain? What do we know?"

Jonah's hand tightened briefly on her shoulder. "She suffered a break in her wrist that required surgery. Luckily, despite her age, she was in perfect health prior to the fall. Although this kind of trauma in an, uh, elderly woman can prove tricky, she's expected to recover fully."

"That woman is our age," harrumphed Aunt Clementine. "Who are you calling elderly, young man?"

Addie snuck a glance up at him as his ears glowed red.

"Speaking strictly clinically, Mrs. Henry falls into that age group."

Hoping to stave off that argument, Addie turned to Jonah. "How do you know this?

He grinned down into her face. "Turns out Mrs. Henry and I share an orthopedic surgeon. I managed to catch Dr. Daniels at the hospital, ask him a few questions."

"Did he wonder why you were asking?"

"Maybe, but he didn't let on. I may have let it slip that she was a very dear friend of my girlfriend's aunts."

"Well played." Grey grinned at Jonah, giving him a thumbs up.

"It didn't hurt that he happens to be a fan of classic cars. Apparently, he's been eyeing their Caddy for years."

"Obviously a man of good taste," cackled Beatrice. "Is he single?" She patted her old lady blue hair helmet.

"Uh, no, he's a married man. Sorry."

"Well, never hurts to ask."

Addie winced at the thought of her aunt trolling for a man thirty plus years her junior. "Maybe we could focus? Did Mrs. Henry say anything to either of you about what happened to her?"

Clementine scooted to the edge of her seat. "Why yes, dear, she did. She complained about hospital food, not having one of your 'bodice rippers,' as she put it, to read. Oh, and something about being pushed. But that might have been the drugs talking."

Shocked silence reigned for a nanosecond before they all started to talk at once.

"Surely, she was wrong," from Aunt Clementine.

"Way to bury the lede," quipped Grey.

Jonah put two fingers in his mouth and whistled. Loudly. Four pairs of eyes turned to him. "One person at a time, starting with me." He turned to her aunt. "Now, Clementine, what did she say exactly?"

Clementine beamed, always enjoying her role as the center of attention. "Well, she insists she didn't fall. Rather irritated about it actually. 'They're treating me like a wobbly old woman' I believe is her direct quote. As she tells it, and to anyone who'll listen, she was starting down the two or three stairs that lead out to the garden. Won't take the ramp, that one, always wants everyone to know how independent she is. Anyway, she swears she felt a thump against her back. And then there she was, lying in a pile at the bottom of the stairs."

"That puts this in a completely different light," murmured Jonah above her.

"So what is this? An angel of mercy creating his own people to 'save?'" asked Addie.

Jonah sank onto the edge of her chair. She glanced at his face, shocked at the granite of it. "Let me be clear. Even if Mr. Hamilton's death is a 'mercy killing' so to speak, it's still murder."

"Mrs. Henry will be so pleased to hear that," commented Beatrice.

"I said 'if,'" Jonah clarified. "We don't *know* what's going on yet. What this does mean is that it's not to be taken lightly. Which means," he leaned forward and made eye contact with everyone before continuing, "no more trips to Magnolia Haven. No more amateur hour. No more sleuthing."

"You can't possibly mean..." Beatrice stopped when his stare hardened.

"I say this with love. Stop."

Addie had to keep her chin from hitting the ground. In all her more-than-she-cared-to-think-about years no one had ever managed to shut up either of her aunts. No one. Another reason to keep him. The list was taller than she was.

Chapter Eleven

Addie stood outside the door. The numbers '144' glowed in the dark, as though the actual numbers were on fire. Silence so thick, it threatened to choke her, permeated the area. And though the temperature soared, she shivered. The only sound was her own heart, thundering in her ears. She gathered her courage around her like an old, beloved blanket and turned to peek into the room. Immediately, she met Mrs. Henry's gaze, her rheumy blue eyes pleading with her. The elderly woman's mouth opened and closed, as though trying to speak with her, but no sound came out. The shadowy figure was nowhere to be seen. Where was he?

"Looking for me?" came a disembodied voice from behind her. Addie shrieked in fear as the cold metal of a needle pierced her neck. The scene around her faded to black as her knees buckled beneath her.

"Addie, honey, wake up." Jonah's

worried tone came to her as though miles away.

She mopped damp curls from her eyes and focused on slowing her labored breathing. Before even opening her eyes, Addie reached out to touch him. The solid warmth of his bicep grounded her, allowed her to break from the nightmare's lingering, icy grip.

"I'm awake," she groaned. "Sort of." The alternative meant she was still trapped in that shadowy hallway. No, thanks!

Jonah leaned down, kissing her. He then scooped her into his arms, saying, "Tell me."

And so she did. They discussed the progress of the dreams, focusing on how the mystery person was able to sneak up on her this time.

"Because you know you're not going to be alone anywhere, right?"

"Yes, sir." She snapped off a mock salute to him.

He put on what she'd come to think of as his solemn face; brows knitted together, eyes dark and staring. "I'm serious, Addie. Deadly serious."

She stroked one hand down over his heavily stubbled jaw. "I know you are, and I promise to be careful." She crossed her fingers across her heart.

Jonah heaved a sigh before smiling into her eyes. "You always say that. And then you always end up in trouble."

"In my defense, I do try to avoid it."

"'Try' being the operative word."

"Can I ask you a personal question?"

He swallowed hard before answering. "Of course you can. Although, I'm a bit terrified at what it might be that you don't know about me already."

She reached up to trace a finger across the eyebrow with the scar dissecting it. "How did you get this? Were you chasing a perp? Did he use a knife? Or maybe a broken bottle?" She shuddered at the thought of someone hurting him.

"Are you sure you want to know? It's not a pretty story." His low, gravelly voice rumbled between them.

Addie gulped and grabbed his hands. "I can take it." She hoped her words were true.

"It was a long time ago, but the...uh...trauma of it remains with me, even today."

"Oh, poor Jonah." She hugged him tightly to her, hoping to ward off bad memories. "Maybe if you tell me, it won't hurt as much anymore."

"Maybe." He drew in a ragged breath. "My sister Maggie burned me with a pan from her toy oven."

Addie pulled back from him, searching his face for the truth, only to have him burst out laughing. "Oh, you bad, bad person. I was so scared!" She pulled the pillow from behind her and smacked him with it.

Jonah, laughing too hard to care, slumped over on the bed. "In my defense, that light bulb was very hot. Singed the hair right off my face. It never grew back."

"I pictured some huge, scary man wielding a weapon. And worse." Although her tone remained strident, she couldn't stop the relief that poured through her.

"What would have been worse than a broken bottle or knife?"

"I don't know for sure, but I'll think of it." Tears rolled down her face, and she angrily brushed them away.

"Hey, hey. Don't cry. You know I can't take it when you cry."

That made her laugh, as she knew he'd hoped. He really couldn't handle her tears. Probably the by-product of growing up the only boy in a flock of sisters.

"I'll stop," she promised, then sniffed a few more times, trying to stop. But the thought of anything happening to him, even years before, set her off. She sobbed against his T-shirt covered-chest.

"So, now you get it," he murmured into her hair. "Now you understand why I beg you to be careful. I can't lose you either."

No words were needed. So, she hugged him a tiny bit harder instead.

*****

Later that morning, while there was the slightest lull in shoppers, Detective Blackwell popped into Smiling Dog Books. Addie schooled her features into her patented you-annoy-me-but-you're-a-customer look. The smile was there but didn't reach her eyes. "Detective Blackwell, what can I do for you? Looking for an early Christmas gift or maybe the latest spy thriller for yourself?"

The detective sidled up to the front counter, and Addie was glad for the barrier in between them. She'd tried to like him; really, she had. He was Jonah's partner after all, but she just couldn't. There was something about him—actually several something—that set her teeth on edge. It may have been his lack of sincerity or innate laziness. Or the way he'd pretty much hit on Erin last month when questioning her about a man who'd come in looking for Addie and wouldn't take no for an answer. Either way, she put up with him. Much like one did with people who wore socks with sandals. Gracey growled low in her throat at Addie's feet. Smart dog!

"Now, how many times have I asked you to call me Dan? After all, we're practically family."

His overly bright smile was meant to put her at ease, she figured, when really it had the opposite effect. She stood as still as a statue, resisting the urge to shudder.

"Okay." Not brilliant, and not what he expected for sure, but all she could manage.

"Jonah isn't here. He had something to do instead of lunch."

"Oh, I know. After all, Jonah and I are tight." He flashed her his patented smile once again. "I was in the neighborhood. Thought I'd check up on you. Since he's 'busy' and all. Anything new happen to upset you?"

"Upset me? You call receiving a death threat 'upsetting'?"

"Now, don't get your panties in a twist. All I meant to do was see if you were okay."

"The state of my panties is none of your concern." *You creepy son of a sailor*, she added in her mind. She felt her cheeks burn but didn't care. "Now, if there's nothing I can help you with, please excuse me. As you can see, I have customers to attend to." It didn't matter that only two single patrons roamed the store. They were getting her very best assistance today.

The fake smile vanished from Dan's face, replaced with the next thing to a snarl. "There's no reason to get snippy." His eyes lingered lower than her face. "See you around. Wouldn't want to keep you from your slew of customers." The detective left the store, slamming the door so hard, the windows rattled.

Addie shuddered before turning to the nearest customer who shot her an uneasy glance. "Guess he didn't like my selection," Addie joked in an effort to put him at ease. "Now, what can I help you find?"

Luckily, the man took the bait and asked

her about some pregnancy books for his wife. She guided him to that section, throwing in which ones her customers preferred. The man, preparing to be a father for the first time, bought all three of her suggestions. Addie rang him up, reminding him that she held story times for toddlers and infants. He left smiling.

Putting the unpleasant experience with Detective Blackwell behind her, Addie turned her attention to helping other customers. She and Jonah had agreed either Grey or Erin would be in the store with her at all times. But, surely running out for a few minutes to grab food didn't count. At least she hadn't thought it did. Now, she wasn't so sure. Grey retuned with their lunches shortly after her run-in. He wasn't at all happy when she told him about it.

"I hope you're going to tell your boyfriend about this," he huffed after listening to her.

"Of course I will. I just hate to do it. They have to work together."

"I get it, but Jonah needs to know. And keep that man on a shorter leash. The nerve of him."

"Agreed. But I'll tell him tonight, in person. I don't want to cause a problem while he's working." She walked away, headed to the reading area to tidy up. Naturally, Grey was right on her tail.

"Maybe we need to add Detective Dumbass to the list."

His words stopped Addie in her tracks, causing Grey to bump into her back. She whirled around.

"Please tell me you're kidding." But the glint in his eye told her he wasn't.

"You've seen how he acts around you. Way too interested, considering you're practically living with his partner."

"I'd never picked up on that."

"Until today."

Addie squirmed under his stare. "You're right. He always struck me as lazy and a bit slimy."

"Kind of like a used car salesman."

"Exactly. It wasn't even so much his words today as the way he kept looking at me. Yuck."

"Jonah is not going to be pleased," Grey gloated.

Addie shook a finger at him. "You don't have to sound so gleeful at the thought."

"Sorry, but now that I'm single, again, I have to live vicariously through you. I can picture it now. That gorgeous hunk of brooding male is going to lose his stuff over this. Ooh, can't wait."

"Well, since I 'll be telling him at home, you don't get a front row seat." Addie stuck out her tongue at him and continued on toward the grouped couches and chairs. She gathered several abandoned books, placing them in a pile, then straightened and fluffed the throw pillows.

"What? How can you be so cruel?" Grey stopped right in front of her. "You know I love a good scene."

"Which is exactly why I won't be telling him in front of you."

"Party pooper," he grumbled like a petulant four-year-old.

"You can stick your bottom lip out as far as it stretches. I'm still not telling him in front of you."

"Fine."

Addie threw back her head and laughed. "Did you remember to order the pies for Thursday?"

"Does a bear know what to do in the woods? I'm not an amateur. I ordered one pumpkin, one mince, one caramel surprise, and turkey-shaped cookies for the girls."

Addie pulled out her phone and opened her notes page. "Great! One more thing checked off for Thanksgiving. What did we ever do before notes pages?"

"Wrote lists on paper?" Grey suggested, tongue firmly in cheek.

"Very funny. You know my brain is Swiss cheese these days. If I don't write it down, forget it."

"And at your advanced age."

"Hey! You're a few months older than me, might I remind you."

"And yet you're the one depending on electronic notes. Although, in your defense, you have a lot on your plate at the moment."

"Yes, thank you, I do." She picked up the stack of books, handing them to him. "Now, earn your keep and put these back where they belong, please."

"Did you forget you don't actually pay me?" Grey asked, moving off toward the shelves.

"I would if you'd accept pay."

"Never. I enjoy my life of leisure."

Addie laughed, shaking her head. It was true. Grey never had to work a day in his life. Although he did do a lot for his family's charitable foundation. But he did spend a lot of time in her store, especially now that she was being threatened by a stalker and had started having the nightmares again. And, as always, she was thankful for his presence in her life. And not just during this, Thanksgiving week.

She looked up as the bells chimed over the door. And nothing could prepare her for the sight of Jonah striding in, anger coming off him in waves. And a stark white bandage across his forehead.

Chapter Twelve

Addie flew to him, her eyes searching frantically for other signs of injury. "What happened to you?" she sobbed before pulling him into her arms.

"A well-aimed rock and some flying glass happened to me. Are you okay?"

"Me? I'm not the one sporting a bandage. Here, sit down. Tell me everything." She led him to the low sofa, all but pushing him into it without ever releasing his hand. "Tell me."

"I was in traffic on the other side of town, stopped at a light actually, when my front passenger window exploded. I was lucky. It's only a small scratch. The medic on scene cleaned me up and used a butterfly to close it."

Addie closed her eyes for a minute. A thousand worse scenarios whipped through her mind like a bad horror movie. And then the realization hit her, the weight of it dragging her down. "It's because of me," she whispered.

She felt his fingers on her chin. "Look at me." He didn't say another word until she opened her eyes. "What happened is not your fault, Addie. Someone doesn't like me very much in this town."

"Someone who likes me a bit too much. It *is* my fault, Jonah. You can't keep getting hurt because of me. I can't live with that."

"And I can't live without you. We will figure this out. I will stop this madness. I promise."

"On a lighter note, it's a good look for you, Jonah. Very dashing." Grey took a seat opposite him. "Did you at least get a good look at the perp?"

Jonah groaned. "Stop watching cop shows. And no, I didn't get a good look. I happened to be glancing out my window when I heard the other one shatter. A piece of brick sat on my passenger seat. Some flying glass caught me, though. I never saw anyone. They're already looking through the video to see if whoever it was got caught on tape." He squeezed Addie's hands. "Not. Your. Fault."

"Good thing you were stopped at a red light," Grey added. "It could have been so much worse." The comment earned him a glare from Jonah and a sob from Addie.

She wiped tears from her face. "Don't you think I've already run through the awful scenarios in my head?"

"Sorry. Filter must be broken today," Grey said by way of apology. He had the grace to duck his head.

"As if you've ever owned one," Addie muttered. She raised her eyes to Jonah. "He's stepping up his game. What can we do?"

"We don't know for sure that this is related to your stalker." He grimaced, whether from the look on her face or that word, Addie wasn't sure. "Really, it doesn't matter. You and I are both at risk. We have to be careful, vigilant."

"I thought we were. I can't, don't, go anywhere alone. I'm never even here alone." She dragged a hand through her short curls. "Don't you see? He's like a terrorist. No, he is a terrorist. They feed on fear. He feeds on our fear. I can't go anywhere alone without wondering if he's out there, waiting for me." She lowered her face into her hands, not even trying to stop the sobs that wracked her body. "I cannot live like this," she muttered through her tears.

Jonah wrapped his arms around her, resting his chin on the crown of her head. He waited until her sobbing lessened, then said, "I know it feels that way right now, Addie, I do. But it won't be forever. Just until we catch him."

She straightened up in time to catch a look pass between the two men. She didn't want to know. Not right now anyway. "And how long will that take, Jonah? I'm losing my mind. This thing has been going on for months. What am I supposed to do? And I've read about stalking on-line. These things can happen for years, Jonah. Years! I don't have years to wait. I want my life back, now."

"I believe he's escalating. I don't think it's going to be very long before he shows his hand, so to speak. Today's incident serves as case in point." He rubbed his head as if just remembering he'd been injured.

An idea started to form in the back of Addie's mind; deep in the shadowy corners. It wasn't an idea Jonah would like or ever go for, but she didn't have a choice. She'd told the truth. She couldn't go on like this for much longer.

Grey leaned forward, elbows on his knees. "This might not be the best time, but we have another problem."

"Grey!" Addie hissed, but it was too late. Jonah was already looking at her, one eyebrow raised.

"Go ahead. You have to tell me now." He sat back in the sofa, finding a more comfortable position but never releasing her hand.

"It's not a big deal." No way did she want to add to the pounding headache he probably already had. She shot Grey a glance. Her patented stop-mud-in-midair one. Not that it ever worked on him.

"Your friend, Detective Do-Wrong, came to chat with Addie today. When he knew you wouldn't be around."

"Grey, I told you I would discuss it with

him." She turned to Jonah. "I wanted to wait until I could tell you in person. Then you came in with that." She pointed at his forehead. "Seems stupid now." She hunched her shoulders, unwilling to add one more thing to the seemingly endless list of their troubles.

"Whatever he did made you feel badly, so it's not stupid. Tell me." Jonah ran a hand along her jaw, pushing her wild curls behind her ear. "Please."

"I'd be happy to tell you all about that...well, you know how I feel about him," Grey groused

"Grey, please," Addie snapped. She sighed and turned to Jonah, telling him about the conversation and the way it made her feel. She watched the muscles around his mouth tighten. "We added him to the list, which I know sounds ridiculous, but you did say anyone who makes me feel uncomfortable."

"I did, and I meant it," Jonah agreed. "I would love to say he isn't our person. And I really don't think he is. Dan is, well, kind of a jerk for lack of a more colorful term, but I don't think he's the stalker. But that doesn't mean I won't be looking at that angle."

Relief coursed through Addie. "Thank you for believing me."

"Did you think I wouldn't?"

"No, not really. I didn't want you to dismiss Dan just because he's another police officer."

"Never. Like everyone else, cops are far from perfect." He shot Grey a quick glance. "He's the only one not being put on the list."

"Because I'm such a wonderful person, right?" He stared at Jonah before bursting out in laughter. "Being gay doesn't hurt either."

"No, it does not," agreed Jonah. He stood, holding out a hand to help Addie off the couch. "Why don't we call it a day? Are you done here for the night?"

Addie glanced around the store. "I'll just come in a bit early in the morning to tidy up. I really want to go home."

Jonah smiled at her. "Me, too. Maybe pick up some pizza on the way home?"

"Home. I like the sound of that."

"Yuck! As cute as you two are, I'm about to fall into a diabetic coma. Have a good night, kids. Don't do anything I wouldn't do." He wiggled his fingers and left.

Addie followed him to the door, locking it behind him. She dimmed the lights and got the girls from behind the counter. Both dogs ran straight to Jonah, crowding in against his legs. She watched as he crouched down to hug both of them. Lily, always the more sensitive of the two dogs, stretched her neck to sniff at the bandage on his forehead. She gave it a quick swipe with her tongue before nudging Addie's hand, as if to say, 'Let's go.'

"I think someone's ready to go home," joked Addie.

"That makes two of us," Jonah agreed.

Several hours later, Addie glanced at Jonah asleep in bed next to her. She brushed his hair back off his forehead and away from the stark white bandage. She'd placed a clean one on after his shower. The long day and dull headache had taken its toll. He lay facing her, his face relaxed in sleep. He'd been out cold for over an hour while sleep eluded her.

Half-formed ideas tumbled through her brain. She needed to end this, once and for all. There had to be a way to draw out whoever stalked her…safely draw him out, she corrected herself. Jonah would never agree to anything remotely putting her in the line of fire. Which was why she couldn't tell him. She hated lying to him, but she hated the idea of his being hurt again, or worse, because of her even more. No, this had to end.

She switched off the lamp and slid down under her comforter. She also had to figure out what was happening at Magnolia Haven and whether or not Mrs. Henry's life was in danger. She'd easily dismissed the older woman's concerns initially, but her nightmares tied it all together. While she didn't understand them, they'd never been wrong. Just vague. She owed the other woman an apology.

Addie tucked the covers around her neck and turned to face Jonah. She lay in the dark, watching him breathe, taking solace from the regular rise and fall of his chest. She placed one hand over his, needing the bond and smiled when his fingers laced with hers. Even in sleep, their connection remained. Yes, she would do whatever she could to end this horror. Even if it meant risking her own safety.

Chapter Thirteen

Wednesday morning, Addie got up before Jonah, showering and getting ready for work before he stirred. She stood at the stove, scrambling eggs when he appeared.

"Morning," he mumbled before heading for the coffee maker.

She turned, hiding a grin at his disheveled hair and the dark stubble on his face. Clearly not a morning person today. "Hey there! Just one more day to go before Thanksgiving," she crowed. "Hope you're ready."

He sipped his coffee before answering, eyes closed as the caffeine hit his system. "From what you've said, not sure I can be ready. But I'll die trying."

She winced before turning back to the stove.

Jonah put his mug down and wrapped

his arms around her. "Too soon to joke about dying, huh? Sorry." He kissed her neck and crossed to the slider, letting the girls in.

"Not sure there'll ever be a good time for that." Her mind raced, looking at her options to catch her stalker from every angle.

"I'm sorry. I was only kidding."

She transferred eggs to two plates, pulling sourdough bread from the toaster. "It's all good. If we can't joke about it, what's the point?"

"True. Cops—really, all the emergency services people I know—are great at gallows humor. Sometimes, too much."

She took a bite of the eggs. "At least with a stalker, I'm never alone."

Jonah stared at her for a long moment. She wondered if she'd gone too far, but then he burst out laughing.

"Not bad for a civilian, right?"

He wiped his eyes with a napkin. "Please don't tell Grey about this conversation. We'd never hear the end of it."

Addie sighed. "It's not funny. Not even a little. Maybe we can reserve these for when this is finally over."

Jonah reached across the table and grabbed her hand, raising it to his mouth. "Of course."

"And one more thing. I don't want to think about any of this for a bit. I'll be careful and all that, but he is not ruining Thanksgiving for me."

"Deal." He kissed her knuckles one more time before digging into his breakfast.

Addie stared at Grey over lunch, wrestling with bringing him into her half-baked idea to catch her stalker. She gnawed her bottom lip.

"I know I'm gorgeous, honey, but you're not my type."

She snickered in response. "I've known that almost as long as I've known you." She picked at her salad; after all, tomorrow was a three thousand calorie day for sure.

Grey sat back, dropping his fork. "You may as well tell me. You know you want to."

"Tell you what? Maybe I was contemplating how lucky I am to have you for my best friend."

"And maybe I'm hitting the road next week as the newest back-up dancer for Prince."

"He's dead."

"Exactly." He narrowed his eyes, continuing to stare at her. "If I didn't know better, I'd think you were plotting something. But you'd never do that without me, right?"

"Not since the great frog incident of nineteen ninety-two."

Grey snorted. "And you would have gotten away with slipping the big ole frog in Miss Hyatt's desk if I'd been there. That meanie never would have suspected nice, little Adelaide Foster."

She laughed until tears streamed down her face. "When you're right, you're right. If only you'd been there to be the lookout. You could have distracted her with your witty ways."

Grey grinned. "Too true. That bat hated me, but a little Wavery charm never hurts." He took a bite of his lunch before continuing. "And as much as I enjoy a great trip down memory lane, don't think you've thrown me off the scent." He smirked.

She shook her head. "You're worse than a bloodhound on the scent."

"Stalling, but true. Out with it."

"I need this to end. This crap where I'm afraid all the time and always looking over my shoulder. I need him caught and put away. I need to get on with my life." She took a breath. "I need to move forward with my life. My life with Jonah. But how can I do that with this hanging over my head?"

"Agreed. What's the plan? Do I get to hurt him? Ooh, we can hide the body. Plenty of places on Waverly land for that!"

Addie blinked back a different type of tears. "You are the very best friend a girl could ever have." She stared at him. "You know that you can't tell Jonah."

"Oh. He really doesn't know?"

She shook her head. "He can't. He'd never agree to it."

"Because he loves you and wants to keep

you safe. Exactly what you want for him."

"Yes and yes. This is wrong." She blew an ebony curl out of her eyes. "And then there's the fact that it may not work. But I can't risk his getting hurt because of me. Not again."

The door opened, and a couple in their twenties strolled in, hand in hand. What it must be to do that, not worrying about someone, or more than one someones trying to kill you, Addie mused. She waved at them. "Welcome to Smiling Dog Books. Let me know if I can help you with anything."

"Thanks," replied the girl. The two wandered to the section containing graphic novels.

Addie leaned across the coffee table. "Here's what I came up with."

*****

Several hours later, the Aunties burst into the bookstore. "Oh my, Mrs. Henry just isn't herself. Addie, you have to do something," Beatrice huffed as she approached the counter.

Addie finished up with a customer, thanking him for his purchase before turning to them. "Tell me everything."

"She looks so old, dear, so very old and sort of shriveled. Like she's shrunk," exclaimed Clementine.

Addie bit her lip to stop from chuckling. Mrs. Henry *was* old, as were her aunts. All three women lived on the downside of eighty-five. "Well, she did have a major trauma and surgery. You can't expect her to be dancing around."

"It's more than that. She's so quiet, lying in her bed like that." Beatrice wrung her hands. "She's withering away."

The two older women babbled amongst themselves, voices reaching a pitch only dogs could hear. Addie tried to interject but couldn't get a word in. Until a shrill whistle broke the fray.

Grey stood behind her aunts, hands on hips. "Ladies, ladies. If I could interject a moment." He waited until all eyes were on him. "Mrs. Henry is not a spring chicken." Grey laughed when Clementine fixed him with her version of 'the evil eye.' "Just stating a fact, my dear."

"It's not too late to uninvite you to tomorrow's feast. And what would Thanksgiving be without my famous sausage and apple dressing?" asked Clementine.

"Or my loved by all, traditional Southern cornbread dressing?" added Beatrice, not to be outshone.

"How is mine not 'traditional?' Grandmother Foster passed that recipe down to me. And she came from a long line of Southern cooks."

"Well, Grandma Bradford was as Southern as pecan pie on Sundays. And she passed that recipe down to me."

Addie would soon have a hole in her cheek from all the biting back of laughter. "Ladies, there's a reason we enjoy two turkeys and two dressings every year. Because both are a required element of the feast." She smiled at both, hugging each. What would she ever do without these cantankerous women? "But maybe we can get back to the subject at hand."

"Oh, of course," exclaimed Aunt Beatrice.

"Yes, we should think of how to help Mrs. Henry. Poor dear," cooed Aunt Clementine.

"Exactly!" Addie interjected. If only she knew how, though. And she surely couldn't tell them about her dreams. Not when their dear friend played the starring role. "We should plan a treat for her, now that she's home. Of course, she won't be able to celebrate Thanksgiving this year, but maybe we could bring it, or a smaller version at least, to her." *And somehow keep her from becoming the next victim,* she whispered to herself.

Clementine glanced at her watch. "Oh my goodness, we have just about twenty-four hours left before the meal tomorrow. Sister, we have to hurry." She bussed Addie's cheek, leaving her in a cloud of eau de lavender, her aunt's signature scent.

"Yes, of course. We have so much to do. See you lovelies tomorrow. Two o'clock sharp." Beatrice hugged Addie before bustling after her sister.

"Grey, we have to write it down. All of

it." The thought of those two women, who'd been the most steadfast pillars of her life, no longer being there resonated as an ache in her soul.

Grey slid an arm around her shoulders, tucking Addie into his side. "We will. Don't worry, we will. The generations to come will hear all the wonderful stories of Clementine and Beatrice." He kissed her curls. "I promise."

She held up one hand, pinkie extended, which he grasped with his. "And no, we don't have to spit or draw blood this time."

"Whew!"

Addie hugged him. "And now, all I have to do is figure out who, if anyone, at Magnolia Haven is a murderer and catch my stalker. In less than twenty-four hours."

"All *we* have to do, you mean."

She smiled at him. "Of course." She slid her phone from her back pocket. "I should at least let Jonah know about Mrs. Henry's condition and the Aunties' plan to bring her dinner tomorrow."

Addie walked into her office to place the call, as Grey had a habit of making noises in the background when she spoke with him. Jonah only had a moment to talk, so she filled him in, leaving out her half-baked plan to catch her stalker. They made plans for a light meal for dinner, in preparation for tomorrow's feast.

Addie sat at her desk and pulled up the 'Web on her phone. Step one of "Operation

Catch the Perv," as Grey had named their plot, commenced. She pulled her Grandmother Foster's engagement ring from her pocket and placed it on her ring finger. She then snapped a picture of it before wrapping it back in cotton and returning it to her pocket. She uploaded the picture to her social media page, changing her status to 'Engaged.' Jonah loathed social media, often citing its role in crime. All those people finding their exes and ruining people's lives. She crossed her fingers and hoped his friends and colleagues shared his beliefs. It didn't matter, as she hoped this might draw out her stalker sooner rather than later. When he was caught and behind bars where he belonged, she'd explain it to Jonah.

Seeing the word 'Engaged' on her profile caused a fluttery sensation in her chest. Not a superstitious person, Addie nonetheless sent a silent prayer to the universe that she hadn't just jinxed herself somehow.

Chapter Fourteen

Thursday morning dawned bright but chilly; perfect Thanksgiving weather. Normally, Addie preferred to muck around the house, watching the Macy's Parade from New York and leafing through the Black Friday ads. She never got to enjoy shopping the next day since opening Smiling Dog Books, but she didn't complain. Business would be brisk. Unlike large retail outlets, Addie believed Thanksgiving should be a holiday spent with loved ones. Eating enough for a small third-world nation. Not shopping. Her store opened bright and early on Friday, and not one second before.

But not today! Today, she was tasked with saving Mrs. Henry. And herself. Friends had pretty much blown up her phone after her fake engagement announcement last night. Thankfully, Jonah hadn't caught on. At least not yet. By the time someone spilled the beans to him, she hoped it would all be a moot point.

The man in question strode into the kitchen, Gracey and Lily prancing around his feet. He raised an eyebrow at the yogurt in her hands. "No hot breakfast today, I guess?"

"Not taking any chances." She was thankful to have slept through the night without any nightmares. "How about you? Want some of this?" She held aloft her yogurt container.

"No, thanks. It feels like a cereal kind of morning." He moved around the kitchen, gathering things. "What are your plans for today? I mean for before the feast?"

"Grey and I are going to spend a few hours in the shop this morning making sure everything is perfect for tomorrow."

She crossed her fingers behind her back, hoping Jonah would forgive her for the small lie. She would be there, after posting something on her shop's social media site making sure everyone who wanted to know about it, did. Grey was at home, whipping up his family's long held recipe for corn pudding; his addition to the already overburdened dining room table at her aunts' home.

"The impending carb coma will prevent me from doing it tonight." *Please don't ask if I need any help.*

"In that case, I might head into work for a few hours. I want to see where we are, if anywhere, with the clues gathered so far. There's something nudging the back of my brain, but I haven't managed to figure it out yet."

"Great!" she yelled, with a bit more enthusiasm than required. "Uh, I mean now I don't have to feel guilty about working for a few hours. If you don't mind feeding the girls, I'll keep them home, since it's only for a little while."

Jonah cocked his head, looking at her intently, as though trying to piece together a riddle. "Okay, then. Shall I meet you back here, or at your aunts' home?"

Addie shoved her hands into the pockets of her robe to stop them from shaking. She was really bad at subterfuge. "Why don't I call you around noon, let you know?' she offered over her shoulder as she rushed to shower.

"Okay," came Jonah's disembodied voice, chasing her into her bedroom.

Addie took the fastest shower ever, rushing by Jonah on her way out the door. One strong hand on her arm stopped her. "Don't I get a goodbye kiss?"

"Of course." Addie kissed him, wondering if deceit held a flavor. "See you in a bit," she called over her shoulder, not making eye contact with him as she left.

Arriving at the bookstore, Addie hustled inside, locking the door behind her and resetting the alarm. She might be taking chances but not that many. She rubbed her fingers at the dull ache in her head and remembered she'd forgotten to take coffee with her. At least she had the small machine in her office. It couldn't create a whipped, caramel anything, but it would have to do.A moment later, the aroma of fresh coffee swirled through the air, waking her further. She sipped the first bit of the steaming liquid when a knock at the front door quickened her pulse. Addie slipped from the back room, approaching the front door with caution. A man's back, partially blocked by the doorframe, greeted her. Wearing a coat and hat, the person was unrecognizable to her.

She took another few steps. "Hello?"

The figure turned, revealing a grinning Detective Blackwell. "Good morning, Ms. Foster. I saw your post about getting ready for tomorrow. Thought I'd come by and see how you were this morning."

His cheerful tone and innocent words did nothing to slow the galloping of her heart. She straightened to her full height, not that it would intimidate him. "I'm fine, thanks. Just busy making the store perfect for tomorrow. Thanks for stopping by." Her neutral tone hid the fear crawling through her.

He stepped closer, jiggling the doorknob with one hand. "Aren't you going to let me in?"

"I, uh, only have a little time before Jonah and I are having dinner with my family. You understand." She gave him a bright smile she didn't feel and turned away. Addie resisted looking over her shoulder as she reached the storeroom, slipping inside. She picked up her abandoned coffee, the hot mug soothing to her now chilly hands, and waited. If Detective Blackwell was indeed her stalker, would her rejection of him push him far enough to act? Minutes crawled by as she waited for some sign. Maybe a brick through the window or noise at the back, employee entrance? But only silence reigned. She knew she had to leave the relative safety of the storage room eventually, so she walked out front. No one stood at the door.

She sighed and glanced around the room. Smiling Dog Books was ready for the onslaught of shoppers in the morning. Bright, shiny book covers caught her eye wherever she looked.

Now what?

Addie made her way to the stool behind the counter. She grabbed a pad of paper and pen, doodling on it. No matter how hard she tried, she couldn't think of anyone to add to the list of potential stalkers she'd given Jonah. She didn't consider her looks stalker-worthy.

Addie swiped to her play list, and Post Modern Jukebox's "Really Don't Care" blasted through the silence. Swaying in time, she struggled to figure out who was making their lives miserable. Each day brought a new host of people one interacts with, from the kid bagging your groceries to strangers you passed on the streets. How could she know?

Crumbling the paper, she tossed it in her recycle bin and thought about Magnolia Haven instead. Surely, that would be easier to figure out. If she'd been there for more than ten minutes and knew any of the staff. Grinding her molars, she couldn't shake the sensation of running out of time. While Mrs. Henry's injury wasn't life-threatening, neither had Mr. Hamilton's illness been. And look how that had ended. The Aunties planned to bring their elderly friend a Thanksgiving treat for dinner, after the much anticipated feast. What if that proved too late?

Addie gathered her purse and keys, hoping the staff she'd met as 'Mrs. Mayberry' had the holiday off. She drove the twenty minutes to the upscale senior residence, formulating a haphazard, Hail Mary plan, and shook her head as she pulled into a parking space. She looked at the clock on her dash; not quite eleven. Plenty of time.

The chilly wind blew her hair in her face as she jogged across the lot. Although the sun shone brightly overhead, the wind had picked up, making it feel much colder than the low forties. By the time she stepped through the front door, she blew on her fingers to warm them. Mitten weather lurked right around the corner.

An older Hispanic woman smiled at her from behind the desk. First lucky break of the day. "Good morning and Happy Thanksgiving! How may I help you?" the woman asked. Her badge read "Mariella".

"Thank you, Mariella, and same to you. I'm here to see my friend, Mrs. Henry."

"Of course! Poor dear is recovering from a nasty spill. Just came back to us from the hospital this week, as I'm sure you know." She pointed to an opened binder on the desk. "If you could please sign in and take one of the visitor badges, please. Mrs. Henry is temporarily staying in our medical wing while she recovers from her accident. Don't worry, she'll receive the best care." She pointed to a hallway to her right. "If you proceed to the end, then take a right, room one hundred forty-four is on your left. Have a nice visit."

Addie stared at the woman, unable to speak after hearing the room number. Just as it had been in her dream. She should be used to this by now. These crazy prophetic dreams had plagued her for months. And then she remembered she was still staring into space. "Thank you."

Addie headed in the direction she'd been told, glancing around her as she went. During their tour of the place, the admissions coordinator had taken them a different way. This hallway appeared darker, less cheerful than the one they'd previously taken. Maybe it was her imagination, but this hallway screamed lost hope and despair. She shook her head. No point in freaking herself out already. At least not any more than she already was.

She passed a nursing station and smiled

at the two women in scrubs who looked up at her from a conversation. Both nodded before looking back down at the paper one of them held. Addie kept walking, trying to ignore the goosebumps covering her arms despite the heat of the building. The further she walked, the darker the hallway seemed to grow. No fresh flowers or paintings on the walls, as she'd seen in the foyer. The gray linoleum flooring showed its age with spots here and scuff marks there. Faded wallpaper sported dreary stripes. She shook her head and kept walking, her footsteps growing more sluggish with each step.

Addie turned the corner and looked up at a sign on the wall. One hundred forty through one hundred forty-five listed for the short hallway. She glanced to the right; sure enough, even numbers lay on that side, just as the receptionist had mentioned. The hall lacked outside windows, depending on dim, overhead fixtures for any light. It may as well have been ten o'clock at night for the darkness. The only other light, faint at best, spilled from the doorway of the last room on the left. Mrs. Henry's room. *Just as it had in her dreams.*

Addie glanced around her, looking for someone. Anyone. But the hall remained empty of patients, staff, or visitors. Surely on Thanksgiving, family would come to visit?

A few drops of sweat streaked down the middle of her back. She moved closer to the wall as she continued toward the last room. Her feet felt as though they were encased in cement. Picking each one up to take another step proved difficult. Keeping her eyes focused on the doorway at the end of the hall, Addie made her way toward it. The faint light grew a little brighter as she did.

The only sound was that of her heartbeat thundering in her ears. She felt in her purse for her phone, grasping it in one, clammy hand. If anything happened, she was ready to dial 9-1-1. She stopped a few feet before the opened door, pressing herself against the wall.

This is real, not a dream.

She repeated the mantra over and over in her head, working up the courage to peer into the room.

Her phone made a turkey call sound, the noise seeming to reverberate off the walls. She gasped and looked at the screen.

Well? What's happening?

This from Grey, who took great pleasure in regularly assigning random sounds and music to her ringtones. She silenced the phone and slid it in her back pocket, holding her breath in a silent prayer that no one had heard it. Frozen in place, she waited, counting to ten in her head. When no one appeared, she crept closer to the door, now just inches away from it.

Addie ran a tongue over her dry lips, but her mouth had grown so dry, it didn't help. Knowing she had to do something, she gathered her courage and resolve, turning into the open doorway. She gasped at the sight that awaited her. Mrs. Henry, looking ten years older than her already advanced age, lay motionless on the bed. She threw one hand over her mouth, stifling a gasp, and rushed to the bedside.

A heavy blanket covered the older woman up to her chin, making it hard to determine if she was even breathing.

"Mrs. Henry?" she called softly, loath to touch her.

Addie had no idea what to do if Mrs. Henry's skin was cold to the touch. She leaned over her further, searching for any sign of life in her too pale face. She held her breath, praying nothing had happened to her friend, when Mrs. Henry's eyes popped wide open. The woman's mouth opened and closed, as though trying to say something, but no sound came out.

Addie jumped back, a startled sound erupting from her throat. She slammed up against something, and started to turn, when a voice asked, "Looking for me?"

She reached for her phone but only had time to shriek in fear before the cold metal of a needle pierced her neck. She struggled against the arms that grabbed her even as the scene faded to black. Her knees buckling was the last thing that registered.

Chapter Fifteen

Cool tile pressed against Addie's cheek, the sensation dragging her up from the depths of sedation. She kept her eyes closed, unsure of her surroundings or the whereabouts of her attacker. Where was she?

Think!

Her mind felt hazy. Her thoughts were jumbled at best. What was wrong with her? A stinging in the back of her neck struck a chord in her memory. Someone had injected her! Who? Why?

Addie cracked her lids a smidgen, trying to see anything around her. A toilet swam into view in the dim light. She tried to bring her hands up to wipe her eyes, but they wouldn't, or couldn't, move. That's when she realized her hands were tied behind her back. Some sort of cotton filled her mouth. She moved her tongue around, trying to dislodge it. Something else had been tied around her mouth, but loosely, and she dislodged it enough to spit out the cotton. Her already dry mouth now felt like the Sahara.

A lone tear dripped from her eye, sliding over her nose and dropping onto the floor. She had no idea of the time, but surely someone missed her by now. She closed her eyes and imagined the scene at the Aunties' home. The delicious scent of roasting turkey would permeate the air. The two sisters would snipe at each other as they rushed around, making last-minute preparations. At some point, Grey would get a wooden spoon to the knuckles after trying to steal a taste. The girls would prance around under foot, ready for any morsel that happened to fall their way. And Jonah would experience his very first Foster Thanksgiving.

Jonah!

Thoughts of him brought more tears spilling from Addie's eyes. Their first Thanksgiving together, and she was somewhere, tied up, lying on a bathroom floor. She gave into her sadness and frustration for a moment, crying silently. She then sniffed and tried to quiet her thoughts. She had to get herself out of here. Grey knew where she was, but she had no idea how much time had passed. Who knew how long he'd wait before worrying and telling Jonah?

Addie wriggled her wrists, trying to figure out what he'd used to bind them. The material scraping across her wrists felt soft, like cotton rather than rope. He probably hadn't been prepared for her coming. Hadn't known he'd be tying up someone. Maybe that could work in her favor. Maybe she had a little time to come up with a plan before he was forced to act. But did Mrs. Henry have that much time?

Not wanting to entertain that thought any longer, Addie bent her knees and tried to swing herself up into a sitting position. After a moment or two of this, all she accomplished was a thick coat of perspiration and the need to vomit. Whatever drug he'd used left her feeling sick to her stomach. The sudden, wild movement wasn't helping. But neither was lying here, feeling sorry for herself. Inching her way across the floor, she pushed her bound feet against the toilet, giving her leverage to slide up the bottom of the wall. After a few minutes of this, she managed to push herself into a seated position.

Sweat poured down her face, and she tried to slow her labored breathing. She really needed to get to the gym more often. Or at all.

Now what?

Addie looked around the tiny bathroom. Was this in Mrs. Henry's room? It must be. Whoever had attacked her wouldn't want to risk carrying an unconscious woman around, would he? She looked around but didn't see her purse anywhere. Where was her phone? A memory of sliding it into her pocket surfaced. She twisted her already painful arms around but couldn't feel anything in the back pocket of her jeans.

Had it fallen when she lost consciousness? Or had her assailant grabbed it?

"Addie, are you there?" came faintly through the mostly closed bathroom door.

Mrs. Henry! She's still alive.

"I'm here, Mrs. Henry. Give me a minute." Spurred on by this new hope, Addie drew her booted feet under her as far as she could and pushed with all her might. She raised to a half-standing, half-crouched position, leaning heavily on the sink. Knowing time wasn't her friend, Addie straightened to her full height and hobbled to the door. Through the dim light, she saw Mrs. Henry, still lying in the bed but head raised. One pale hand beckoned to her, signaling her to stop.

That's when Addie heard footsteps outside the room.

He's back!

Knowing time had run out for both of them, Addie hopped toward the door, throwing her weight against it. A loud yelp was followed by something clattering to the floor. A needle lay next to her. The door opened enough for the man to pull out his arm, and Addie slammed back against it, closing the door with him on the outside. She nudged a chair with her hip, wedging it under the doorknob. That might buy them a little time.

"Mrs. Henry, you have to help. We only have a few seconds. Do you have a phone? Call nine-one-one. Now!"

Seconds became hours as the elderly woman leaned toward the bedside table, her shaking hand reaching for the phone that sat there. Addie held her breath as she tried to grab it, but the phone clattered when she knocked it to the floor. Mrs. Henry lurched to grab it, almost toppling out of the bed.

"Stop! The last thing you need is another fall."

"I was pushed," came her tremulous reply.

A wave of nausea rolled over her. "Be sure to mention that to the police. Right now, we have to get to the phone."

Addie lowered herself to the floor and scooted across it on her butt until the phone lay just behind her. Blindly reaching out, her fingers grasped the older model phone.

"A little to your left, dear," called Mrs. Henry from above her.

Addie's fingers pressed on the bottom part of the phone. The dial tone was sweet music to her ears. "Now if I can just dial nine-one-one," she muttered. Perspiration dripped into her eyes, burning them as she traced the rows of numbers, seeking the ones she needed.

After what felt like an eternity, a woman's voice called out, "Nine-one-one, what is the nature of your emergency?"

Before Addie could answer, the elderly woman bellowed from the bed, "Some rude young man is trying to kill us. That is the nature

154

of the emergency. We are at Magnolia Haven, 12004 Magnolia Lane, and we require some assistance. Preferably of the police variety."

"Ma'am, what's going on exactly?"

The sound of her attacker trying to break into the room sent adrenaline through Addie's veins. "There is a man here trying to kill both of us. Do you hear that?" She swung to face the door, addressing her attacker. "Do you hear that? We're on the phone with the police. It's too late for you!"

"Ma'am, who are you talking to?" the dispatcher asked

"That's right, you slimy miscreant. Picking on people you think can't fight back. I'll show you."

"Hello?" came the voice on the phone.

All the yelling only increased the pounding in Addie's head. "Please hurry. Someone drugged me and tied me up. He's outside the door trying to get in. You have to hurry." She gave the dispatcher her name.

"I have a car in your area. He should be there in under two minutes."

Addie hoped they had that long. "We're in room one forty-four, all the way in the back of the first floor."

"Where they put the sick, old people," added Mrs. Henry. "I'm only here because I broke my wrist."

Addie backed up across the floor, putting all her weight against the door. "Did you hear that? The police are on their way."

"Her boyfriend is Detective Jonah Wolfe of the Ocean Grove Police Department. Someone better inform him of this. He'll want to know," Mrs. Henry added.

Addie would have lowered her aching head into her hands, if they weren't tied behind her back. Jonah was going to be so angry with her. Suddenly, the only sound in the hall was that of running feet. And then a body falling to the floor. And some grunting.

"Are the police here already? It sounds like a scuffle in the hallway," Addie asked the dispatcher.

"No, ma'am, they're just pulling in now. I'm not sure what you're hearing."

The door shook hard against her back. "Addie, are you in there? Let me in!"

Relief flooded through her system and she rolled away from the door. "Jonah, thank goodness," she cried as she kicked the chair from under the doorknob.

She rolled further from the door, allowing Jonah and Grey to run into the room. She craned her neck to see someone in scrubs lying still on the floor.

"Is he, uh, out?"

"As in unconscious? You bet!" Grey laughed as he announced this.

Jonah swept her up off the floor and into his arms, his dark eyes, and expression, unreadable. "Are you okay?" he asked in a huskier than normal voice.

"I'm fine. Or I will be. Did I miss dinner?"

A laugh burst from him as he clutched her to his chest. "What am I going to do with you?" he muttered in her ear.

"Don't worry, we saved you some," answered Grey from next to the hospital bed.

"You didn't seriously start without me?" Addie wailed.

Any answer was cut off by two uniformed officers rushing through the door. Jonah turned to fill them in, gesturing to the man on the hallway floor. He then gently set her from him and unwound the gauze bandaging tying her wrists together. He kissed the chafed skin beneath, bringing tears of another type to her eyes. She swung her legs around so he could undo them as well.

He placed a hand under her chin, raising her gaze to meet his. "I'm so glad you're okay. Yet another thing to be thankful for today."

"You and me both."

"Let's get you out of here."

"Sounds like a plan." He helped her up and held onto her as her wobbly legs gained some strength. Addie moved over to the bed. "You were amazing," she whispered to the older woman. Color returning to Mrs. Henry's skin brought a smile to Addie's face.

"Not so bad yourself, young lady. We make a great team."

Addie kissed her cheek. "I'll see you very

soon. In fact, I'll come back tomorrow with some books for you to read."

"Make sure they have a half-naked man on the cover!" Mrs. Henry cackled.

"Of course." Addie allowed Jonah to lead her out of the room. He'd have a thing or five to say to her about her reckless behavior, but that was okay. Beat the alternative.

Epilogue

Jonah groaned before leaning back in his chair.

"Can't say I didn't warn you," Addie teased.

He raised his linen napkin and waved it like a flag. "I surrender."

"What? Not before you sample some of my famous bourbon sweet potato pie, young man," crowed Aunt Clementine from one end of the table.

Aunt Beatrice, not to be outdone, thumped her hand on the table-top. "Right after he's sampled some of my delicious pecan and pumpkin bread pudding."

"Would this be a good time to throw my traditional pumpkin layer cake into the ring?" asked Gertie, eyes twinkling with laughter.

Jonah threw up his hands. "I'm happy to

try them all, ladies, but maybe after a nap?"

Addie sat back and looked around the table. All the people she loved had gathered here, the evening after Thanksgiving, to celebrate the holiday. After a short stay in the ER to check on the effects of the sedative used to drug her, she'd spent several hours with the police, telling and retelling her story.

It seemed the suspect, one Brian Clarke originally from Alabama, had lost his nursing job in that state after the questionable death of two of his elderly patients. Local police had never found enough proof to charge him, and Brian had slipped away to start over. And now his nursing days were over.

He'd come to in the back of an ambulance, telling everyone who'd listen that he was an 'angel of mercy' sent to relieve others of their Earthly suffering. Jonah grumbled that he'd better be found competent to stand trial and answer to what he'd done. And tried to do to Addie.

Her stalker remained a mystery, at large to terrorize her in any way he saw fit. But, for tonight at least, she'd put that thought aside. Tonight, she would bask in the warmth of these people she loved so dearly.

They continued to grumble, comparing desserts. Grey offered to eat all of them if Jonah couldn't 'man up.' That brought a giggle to her lips.

She raised her wine glass, which

contained ginger ale thanks to yesterday's incident. "A toast to all the wonderful people in this room. I love each and every one of you."

"Some more than others," Grey teased.

"Maybe not more, just different. And I am so very thankful to be here with you all today."

"Here, here," agreed Aunt Clementine, raising her glass of bourbon. No fruity wine for her, as she liked to say. "And to any little Fosters who might join us in the future." She looked at Addie over her reading glasses. "After all, young lady, you're not as young as you used to be."

"And neither are your eggs," added Aunt Beatrice, not to be outdone.

Jonah squeezed her hand, grinning at the odd toasts. Everyone raised their glasses, laughing as they drank to her eggs.

Only in this family, Addie thought.

And she wouldn't have it any other way.

The End

ALSO BY
KIMBERLEY O'MALLEY

COZY MYSTERIES
The Addie Foster Series
Book 1: Death Comes in Threes
http://bit.ly/KOMcozy1
Book 2: Dyeing for Change
http://bit.ly/Addie2KOM
Book 3: Murder by Numbers
http://bit.ly/AddieBook3

CONTEMPORARY ROMANCES
The Windsor Falls Series
Book 1: Coming Home
http://bit.ly/ComingHomeKOM
Book 2: Taking Chances
http://bit.ly/TakingCHancesKOM
Book 3: Second Chances
http://bit.ly/2ndChancesKOM
Book 4: Saving Quinn http://bit.ly/SavingQuinn
Book 5: Finding Kat http://bit.ly/FindingKat
Book 6: Coming Back
http://bit.ly/FInalWindsorFalls

ACKNOWLEDGMENTS

This is my tenth book in just under three years. Tenth! Oh and two anthologies as well this year. Needless to say, I've been a busy, little bee. But of course, none of this was possible without my amazing team!

Rebecca Pau of The Final Wrap is my brilliant cover designer, whom I love so very much. She always knows just what I want, and need, without my having to say it. Which is a good thing, as I'm terrible at putting my vision for my covers into words. Thank you for yet another gorgeous cover!

Margie Greenhow, PA extraordinaire, keeps me in line and on track. She nudges, cajoles, and sometimes shoves me into new adventures and undertakings. And I am a better person for it. Thank you!

Every author thinks they're brilliant. And then they think everything they write is pure...you get the idea. And that's why we have editors; people to keep us from slitting out wrists. And I'm lucky enough to have a few. Thank you to Karen Boston and Chelly Hoyle Peeler. You guys have a tough job.

Molly, my Shetland Sheepdog, is the inspiration for Gracey and Lily. Molly is my third child. Somedays I like her more than I do my human ones. She's always there at my side, with a lick or a woof to encourage me.

And, always, there's my family! They are at the center of everything I do.

HOW TO HELP AN INDIE AUTHOR

Thank you for reading Angel of Death. I know you have millions of books to choose from, so thank for choosing mine.

So, here's one more favor...reviews, reviews, reviews! Even if you didn't fall in love with this book, please take the time to review it on Amazon, Goodreads and/or Book Bub. Reviews are so much more important than you could ever imagine.

ABOUT THE AUTHOR

Kimberley O'Malley is a transplant to Charlotte, North Carolina from the frozen North. She is learning to say y'all but draws the line at sweet tea. Sarcasm is an art form in her world. She writes small town Contemporary Romances and hilarious Cozy Mysteries. When not writing, she is a full-time nurse and part-time soccer Mom, but not necessarily in that order. She shares her life with an amazing husband of more than 23 years, two teenagers, and one very sweet Shetland Sheepdog, Molly.

To ensure you're up to date with all the shenanigans and news, visit the link to follow along with my monthly newsletter: http://eepurl.com/dgonEX

ARE YOU FOLLOWING THE AUTHOR?

Facebook -
https://www.facebook.com/KOMalley67/

Instagram -
https://www.instagram.com/kimberleyomalley67/

Twitter - https://twitter.com/K_OMalley67

Website - www.kimberleyomalley.com

Amazon Author Bio -
www.amazon.com/author/kimberleyomalley

Good Reads Profile - http://bit.ly/grKOM

Book Bub Profile - http://bit.ly/bookbubKOM

www.ingramcontent.com/pod-product-compliance
Lightning Source LLC
Chambersburg PA
CBHW060822120626
46557CB00001B/335